"A great man has come into your life."

The old woman bent over Heather's hand, muttering softly. "Ah. He is a stranger. Tall and dark. You will marry, and together, you will gain all the world has to offer."

Heather had to smile; fortune-tellers all sounded alike. Besides, she could have told the Gypsy that Branko's father was the only stranger she'd met. And she hardly considered Nick Antonovic a "great man!" In fact, just remembering their argument brought a wave of heat to her face.

The Gypsy's eyes narrowed. "You don't believe Zamura, but I will tell you one last thing. This man will be the only great love of your life."

Heather grimaced. "Well, thank you for the reading," she managed lightly. To her irritation, images of Branko's handsome—and autocratic—father passed through her mind again. "Zamura," she ventured, holding out her arm, "would you help me undo the bracelet?"

"I cannot! It is a sign. And I cannot interfere with the signs...."

Rebecca Winters, an American writer and mother of four, is a graduate of the University of Utah, who has also studied overseas at schools in Switzerland and France, including the Sorbonne. She is currently teaching French and Spanish to junior high school students. Despite her busy schedule, Rebecca always finds time to write. She's already researching the background for her next Harlequin Romance!

Books by Rebecca Winters

HARLEQUIN ROMANCE
2953—BLIND TO LOVE
3047—FULLY INVOLVED
3090—THE STORY PRINCESS
3120—RITES OF LOVE
3144—BLACKIE'S WOMAN

THE MARRIAGE BRACELET

Rebecca Winters

Harlequin Books

TORONTO • NEW YORK • LONDON
AMSTERDAM • PARIS • SYDNEY • HAMBURG
STOCKHOLM • ATHENS • TOKYO • MILAN
MADRID • WARSAW • BUDAPEST • AUCKLAND

Dedicated to all my dear friends
in Spokane—with fond memories of those
wonderful boating days!

ISBN 0-373-03192-0

Harlequin Romance first edition April 1992

THE MARRIAGE BRACELET

CHAPTER ONE

"Ms. MARTIN, we can talk for a moment. Yes?" implored a voice in heavily accented English.

Heather Martin smoothed a swath of ash-blond hair away from her face, surprised to discover Branko Antonovic hadn't left the classroom with the other students. He knew she didn't have time to give extra help once the lesson was over, and she'd already spent half an hour before class trying to teach him the difference between transitive and intransitive verbs.

During the fall term, the eighteen-year-old Gypsy immigrant from Yugoslavia had needed so much help with English that she'd made arrangements to tutor him privately, without any thought of payment. Heather was licensed to teach citizenship and ESL— English as a second language—in two states. Weekdays she taught in Spokane, Washington. But twice a week she traveled to nearby Priest River, Idaho, where she taught evening ESL classes; she made a point of arriving an hour or so early to give Branko some individual attention. They often sat outside on the school steps to chat for a few minutes first, and whenever they did, Branko smoked several cigarettes in quick succession. He always complained good-naturedly about not being allowed to smoke at work, at school or even at home.

In the beginning she'd lost patience with him because he continually pestered her for a date and didn't take their study sessions seriously. From personal experience she had learned that a certain amount of hero worship on the part of recent immigrants toward their English teachers sometimes came with the territory. But Branko's infatuation had forced her to deliver an ultimatum. Either he settled down and took the work seriously, or he'd have to finish his ESL classes with another teacher—which meant traveling to another town much farther away.

To her relief, her warning had produced the desired effect. Overnight he became the model student and set about impressing her with his ability to learn English. For the past six months he had made steady progress; in a few more years he'd be ready to take his citizenship test, a feat Heather's predecessor, Mrs. Wood, would never have imagined.

According to Mrs. Wood, who had retired early to take care of her ailing husband, Branko came from Slovenia at the age of seventeen, speaking Romany, the tongue of the Gypsies. Heather had never taught a Gypsy before and quickly learned that, though the language was Indic in origin, it had evolved as the Gypsies moved across Asia and Europe. Branko's particular dialect included many Slavic words. However, he could neither read nor write, so he had to be taught English the same way one would teach a child who had never been exposed to formal schooling, a formidable challenge at best.

As time passed, Heather came to the conclusion that Branko was naturally bright. But that first month his flirtatious behavior tended to blind her to his academic potential, and for a while, she was afraid she'd made a mistake in taking on the private sessions. The fact that she was nine years older than Branko didn't seem to disturb him. Perhaps it was because she looked closer to twenty than twenty-seven, and he appeared older and acted more mature than most of his eighteen-year-old American counterparts. Heather recognized the appeal his dark melancholy eyes and unruly black hair would have for the opposite sex, especially as he grew older.

But of course she kept those thoughts to herself. What she did tell him was that she never allowed herself to become personally involved with her students. Such behavior was unethical and could cost her her job.

She went on to explain that she'd been teaching for six years and felt a strong, binding link with all her students. But she drew the line at anything beyond class parties and cultural activities, and told Branko the extra attention she was giving him before class sprang from a desire to help him improve his English, nothing more. Apparently her talk convinced him, because from that point on, he settled down and began to excel.

The class of seven included two Mexicans, a Laotian, a Cambodian, an East Indian, an Iranian and Branko, who also happened to be the youngest. Heather had nothing but admiration for her students, who worked hard during the day to earn a living, yet at night found time to attend classes and do the required studying.

In their place, Heather wondered if she could ever have managed as well or been able to tackle another language so foreign to her mother tongue. Not only did she feel compassion for Branko, with his unique background and language problems, his impeccable behavior had endeared him to her during the past six months. She smiled at him. "What did you want to ask me, Branko?"

He formed the words with some difficulty. "You come to Priest Lake—" he paused "—Sunday. Three o'clock. Yes?" Then he produced a sheet of paper from his sleeve with a magician's flourish, which left Heather chuckling as she smoothed it out on the desk. Next to a makeshift map he'd printed an address in uneven block letters. She wasn't sure he'd ever master cursive and thought at this stage he was doing well to be printing legibly.

When she looked up at him, he had already anticipated the question forming on her lips. "We have celebration. The day of St. George."

She had never heard of it. "Is this a Romany custom?" she asked, her interest growing. His Gypsy background intrigued her, and she'd already learned quite a lot from him.

Branko nodded, his black eyes alive with excitement. "Very important. You come, please?"

The wistful plea, earnestly uttered, touched a vulnerable spot inside Heather. If Branko had close friends, she wasn't aware of it. He always came to school alone and left alone. As far as she could tell, he didn't socialize with the other students outside of class, though she supposed that was understandable because they were all older. But even if they'd been the same age, she had a feeling he wouldn't mix with them. Branko seemed to be a troubled young man. Maybe that was why he smoked one cigarette after another....

Several negative references to his father, Nick Antonovic, had let her know his home situation left a lot to be desired. As macho as he pretended to be, she sensed a certain loneliness in him and a discontent that, strangely enough, made her want to reach out and comfort him. No student had ever made her feel quite this protective before. She supposed it stemmed from some latent maternal instinct, coupled no doubt with the painful fact that, due to a recent illness, she would never be able to have children.

She stared at the paper. Occasionally she and the other ESL teachers in the region attended various religious or holiday celebrations of their students. Heather enjoyed learning about their lives and had a genuine interest in their backgrounds. She found it helped her understand them better, and understanding was the key to success in the classroom.

She reasoned that she ought to attend this Romany festival because it seemed so important to Branko. The opportunity to meet his family and find out if there was any other way she could help him integrate into society provided the impetus.

She wouldn't have any trouble locating the site. For years her family had water-skied at Priest Lake, a large beautiful body of water dotted with islands and surrounded by pines and sandy beaches. Boaters and campers alike found it a veritable paradise.

A thoroughfare connected it to Upper Priest Lake, a wilderness area she had explored dozens of times with her older brother, Jay. They were championship water-skiers, and until the year before when a severe bout of endometriosis had put her temporarily out of commission they had won every slalom skiing competition in the Pacific Northwest.

As far as Heather was concerned, Priest Lake would make an ideal site for a celebration. She could picture an encampment of Gypsy caravans near the shore. Branko probably lived in one.

She tapped the paper against her cheek, deep in thought. Branko didn't press her. He simply eyed her with that soulful expression of his. When she smiled, he grinned back and she found she didn't want to disappoint him. If the truth be known, she wanted to learn more about his fascinating heritage. Long before meeting Branko, Heather had been curious about Gypsies.

Her father owned a thriving chain of fabric stores throughout the state of Washington. His main store in Spokane was only doors away from a Gypsy tearoom. A few of the Gypsy women came in to her father's shop at least once a week to buy fabric and trims. And Heather, who helped out on Saturdays and during the summer, always dropped what she was doing to wait on them.

At first, the Gypsy women, who spoke Romany among themselves, seemed like a closed society to her and didn't engage in the small talk she tried to initiate. Undaunted, Heather continued to go out of her way to help them. Little by little, as she offered suggestions and anticipated their predilection for bright colors, lustrous textures and sequins, they lowered their guards. Once in a while she could get them to smile and talk to her. Perhaps she'd recognize some of them at this St. George Day, she thought now. Gypsies in the region would probably band together for a holiday celebration.

"I'll tell you what, Branko. I think I can come. I'll try. Do you understand?"

"Yes." He nodded his dark curly head. "I search for you."

She smiled. "You mean, I'll *look* for you. Remember we had that lesson last week."

"No," he told her in a serious voice. "I look *at* you. Bu-tee-ful," he said, struggling to get it right. Then he winked.

"You pronounced that word very well," she responded, ignoring his playful charm. It was the best way to handle Branko. "Thank you for the invitation."

"You are welcome," he returned quickly, sounding as though he'd memorized the come back line. "You not forget."

"You *won't* forget," she corrected him.

"I won't forget." This was one time she couldn't tell if he was teasing or not. "Three," he said firmly, lifting three fingers for emphasis, studying her with somber eyes. At other times, his eyes were coal-dark fires of passion and mischief, leading her to believe he had nothing of importance going on in his head. Occasionally they were filled with pain.

Therein lay the trouble. Branko Antonovic was an enigma. Heather had a difficult time keeping up with his mercurial moods because she didn't have the slightest idea what had precipitated them.

"Three," she said. "I'll try to make it. Good night, Branko."

He stared at her with a glimmer of satisfaction glowing in those dark eyes before he dashed from the room. Once he'd left, she looked down at the rumpled paper, wondering about his parents. Why weren't they taking classes, too? She assumed they'd all come over from Yugoslavia together, so why hadn't she met them before?

Mrs. Wood hadn't known anything about his parents, either. Before Heather had taken over the older woman's classes, the two of them had spent several days discussing the students and their individual problems.

But Branko remained a mystery. All Mrs. Wood could tell Heather was that he'd been "mainstreamed" with the seniors at the high school to pick up English. After graduation, the district supervisor had placed Branko in Mrs. Wood's night class. Her only personal comment about Branko had been that he was a loner.

The idea of meeting his people on Sunday appealed to Heather. Perhaps she could encourage them to accompany him to the classes, since very often ESL became a family affair. If tuition was a problem, the school had an emergency fund.

Gathering her notebook and papers, she turned off the lights and left the school to head back to Spokane in the new Wagoneer she'd purchased the previous month. At first, an Alfa Romeo Spider had caught her eye, but she'd had to rule it out as impractical. It only held two people and couldn't pull the family boat.

The Wagoneer, on the other hand, had already proved its worth. Only the Saturday before, she and Jay had taken their vans to pick up her ESL students at the school in Priest River, along with any family members able to attend. They'd driven them to her house in Spokane for a waterskiing party and barbecue. She'd hoped to meet Branko's parents, but apparently they hadn't been able to attend; when she asked him why, he merely shook his head, eyebrows lowered mutinously.

The party had turned out to be a success, primarily due to Branko. He surprised Heather and Jay, as well as everyone else, by getting up on two skis and staying up, something none of the others could do. Their admiration for his prowess broke the ice, and for the first time since she could remember, Heather watched him respond favorably to their attention. Towards the end of the evening, Branko was helping some of the others, a gesture that pleased Heather.

When asked where he'd learned to ski, Branko shrugged, indicating that he'd just picked it up. Part of his macho image. But Heather knew otherwise. Someone had taught him how to ski off a pier and call out instructions when he wanted the boat driver to "hit it."

Jay happened to be at the helm while Heather stood in the back of the boat letting out the rope. She smiled now, remembering the look of surprise that had flashed between her and her brother. It said this was a new side to the young Gypsy who kept too much to himself. Heather had confided to her brother her concerns for Branko, his seeming isolation, his moodiness.

Letting out a tired sigh, she stepped on the gas, anxious to get home to bed. Too many late nights commuting and grading papers had worn her out. Though fully recovered from her illness, she seemed to require more sleep than before. The doctor had said this would pass, but Heather was impatient to feel like her old self again, a woman with enough energy for a dozen people.

Normally she didn't mind the hour's drive back to Spokane. It gave her time to make lesson plans for her day classes at the community school. But tonight, as she sped along the forest-lined road, her thoughts dwelled almost exclusively on Branko.

More and more she liked the idea of attending the celebration. For one thing, she could try out some of the Romany words Branko had taught her. She'd made an effort to learn a few fundamental concepts of all the languages spoken by her students, so that she could better appreciate their particular difficulties studying English. But Romany fell into a category all its own.

Some people referred to it as the "secret language." She could understand why, since it had no written base and was spoken only by Gypsies. Each tribe had developed its own version, borrowing words from the local language. Heather knew that the Gypsy women who visited her father's store were originally from eastern Europe, like Branko. She hoped to see them on Saturday; perhaps they'd let her practice her pitifully short list of Romany words on them. That way, she'd sound more confident when she greeted Branko's family at Sunday's festival.

Twenty minutes later she pulled into the driveway of her parents' home, a spacious ranch-style home by the Spokane River. She'd been living with them ever since her release from the hospital. Her parents had urged her to give up her apartment in town until she was fully recovered. Because she'd been too weak and despondent at the time to argue with them, Heather had submitted to her parents' wishes. But now she felt fine; not only that, she'd saved enough money for a down payment on a condominium. She planned to move in before the end of the summer.

In the meantime, her parents were delighted to have her home again, and Heather was equally delighted to assist with the housework or in the store. And this particular weekend, she looked forward to seeing the Gypsies there.

But although the store was crowded with shoppers enjoying the unseasonably warm June weather, she saw no sign of the women. Neither did the manager, who'd been keeping a lookout for them.

Since the celebration was probably a regional event, the Gypsies might already have gone to Priest Lake in anticipation of the festivities. Later in the day, when she passed the Gypsy tearoom on the way to her car, the Closed sign propped in the window confirmed her suspicions.

Sundays always meant a big dinner and a family get-together at the Martin home. Jay was married and the proud father of a baby girl. He and his wife, Shelley, usually came over after church and ate dinner with Heather and their parents.

However, because of Branko's invitation, Heather decided not to eat until she got to the festival. It would take her an hour and half to get there, so she had to leave soon after the others arrived. She gave her baby niece, Stacy, a quick squeeze, then headed off.

"Hey, Hez. Wait up!" Jay called, following her to the back door, which led into the garage. He was as blond as Heather and had the physique of a tennis player. "Feel like company?"

"What?" She whirled around, surprised at her brother's suggestion.

"At the ski party, Shelley and I had the impression that Branko's more than a little infatuated with you. We saw him eyeing you when you were helping the others with their skis. It was a calculating, possessive look, if you know what I mean."

She shook her head. "He got over that months ago, Jay."

"Don't count on it."

She flashed her brother a wry smile. "I'm twenty-seven now. I think I can look after myself.

He threw up his hands in defeat. "You're right. Have a good time."

"I'm sure I will," she said as she climbed into her car. "I'd like to meet his parents and let them know

I'm proud of the progress he's been making. I told you he never had any formal education until he started attending Priest River High School last year. Since he invited me, I think he'll feel slighted if I don't come." She waved and began to back out of the garage. "See you later."

Heather couldn't help smiling, because every once in a while Jay still enjoyed playing big brother. She supposed it was inevitable. He tended to be protective, and as they were only eleven months apart, they'd always been close, not only liking many of the same things, but often experiencing a kind of mental telepathy. Heather's father had often joked that, until Heather found a man she liked better than Jay, she would never get married. Maybe it was true.

She left Spokane and drove north, relaxing to some classical music while she enjoyed the beauty of the fabulous summer day. The sky was an intense blue and the temperature had soared into the high eighties.

On the outskirts of Priest River, she passed a string of cars and proceeded to attract the attention of three young men in a truck pulling a boat. They couldn't have been a day over eighteen, but were whistling and calling her to follow them. She grinned and shook her head. With the navy chiffon scarf knotted beneath her shoulder-length blond hair, she probably looked younger than she was, especially from a distance. Besides, at this time of year, any female was fair game to the droves of male boaters and water-skiers jamming the highways to get to the lakes.

Leaving them far behind, she soon reached the turnoff for Priest Lake, but the traffic forced her to reduce her speed. At this rate, her sleeveless white linen dress would be creased and limp when she finally arrived.

A glance in the mirror told her she'd need to touch up her lipstick. Aside from that, she wore no other makeup. The dark brows and lashes that framed velvety brown eyes inherited from her mother made a startling contrast to her Scandinavian coloring.

Soon the main boat-ramp area came into view. Escaping the crowd, she veered to the right and wound her way along the lake road, where some of the more luxurious private homes could be glimpsed through the pines.

An address on a mailbox told her she was close to her destination, and this surprised her, because only the well-to-do could afford to live on this particular stretch of lakefront property.

She finally stopped near a private driveway that disappeared into a copse of pines. The address was the same as the one printed on the paper she pulled from her purse.

Since the Gypsies liked to keep to themselves, it was possible they'd arranged to hold their celebration on private land, away from other people. She took a few moments to run a brush through her tangled hair and apply a frosted pink to her lips, trying to make herself presentable before starting down the road.

When she came upon a chalet-style house tucked away in the forest, her eyes widened in surprise. It was too large for a cottage, yet because of the wildflowers painted on the shutters, it reminded her of homes she'd seen in the Alpine meadows of Europe when she'd traveled there.

Enchanted by the sight, she lost track of time, and several minutes passed before she realized there were no people about, no signs of a celebration. Only a Jeep parked in the drive signaled the presence of anyone else.

She glanced at her watch. It was ten after three. Growing more and more perplexed, she got out of her car and walked along the stone path toward the stairs that led to a sheltered porch. Wooden tubs of flowering ranunculuses in vibrant yellow stood at either side of the front door.

She hoped there would be someone home who could point her in the right direction. Surely Branko hadn't made a mistake about the address, considering the occasion had seemed so important to him.

When she couldn't find a bell, she lifted an ornately carved wooden knocker that looked very old and foreign. On closer inspection she could see it resembled a bouquet of wildflowers like the ones on the shutters, exquisitely shaped to the smallest detail.

Heather felt the carving with the pad of her thumb and wondered about the person responsible for such artistry before tapping the knocker against the door. When there was no answer, she tried again.

Suddenly the door opened, and a Branko she had never seen before stood in the entry. Instead of his usual garb, the American jeans, T-shirt and black leather jacket he wore to class, he had put on a cream satin shirt, open almost to the waist and tucked into black pants belted by a crimson sash. The unfamiliar clothes emphasized his swarthy complexion and, of course, his fascinating Gypsy heritage.

Around his neck he wore a chain with some kind of gold coin dangling from it. Several ornate rings adorned his fingers. But what transformed him most of all was the soft black fedora that crushed his dark curls around his forehead, giving him a wild exotic look.

"Come in, please." He imitated what he had learned in class perfectly, and making a deep bow, swept off his hat, but Heather didn't move. Something was wrong, though she couldn't immediately put her finger on it.

"When you wrote down the address, I had no idea this was your home. Where is the festival, Branko? I don't see any people."

He trained guileless black eyes on her. "You taste a drink from my country first. Yes?"

Heather expelled a sigh, recognizing that Branko was being evasive. "Are your parents here? I'd like to meet them."

He hunched his shoulders. "My *dej*—my mother," he said, "she is dead." Unbelievably, tears welled in his eyes. The display of emotion was so unexpected, it struck a responsive chord in Heather. No wonder Branko had seemed so unhappy at times.

"I'm sorry, Branko."

He blinked, and one tear coursed down his cheek. "My *dad* make me come here to start a new life," he said, pronouncing the Gypsy word for father in the Romany way, with an "ah" sound. "But he is, how you say it, very upset because she die. He is all the time angry. I not like him. Please. You want to come in?''

She couldn't refuse. ''Yes, of course I do.'' Not wishing to add to his distress, she followed him inside, pondering the revelation that he'd lost his mother and was obviously unhappy about living with a grieving father.

The situation would explain the emptiness often mirrored in his eyes. How on earth had his father come to Idaho, of all places? Was he an American citizen? Was that the reason he hadn't come to ESL class with his son? And how had he made the kind of money to own property and build a home like this?

''I can't stay long, Branko. You do understand that I have at least an hour-and-a-half drive back to Spokane after I leave the celebration?''

He nodded as if her reminder was totally unnecessary, then closed the door and showed her through a large entry hall to a living room furnished in a traditional European decor. Her gaze was drawn to the highly polished chairs and cabinets hand-carved from dark wood. The superb view of Priest Lake was the only thing that told her she was still in Idaho.

One particularly magnificent painting of jagged mountain peaks covered in snow caught her attention. It dominated the wall above the carved wooden fireplace inlaid with antique-looking tiles. ''What a wonderful house,'' she murmured in awe. Turning to Branko, she asked, ''Are those the Alps in Yugoslavia?'' Her glance returned to the painting.

''A-a-p-s?'' He tried to pronounce the *l* but failed, then he shrugged. He rolled his eyes and held up three fingers. "My *papo* live... did live there," he said, gesturing at the painting. "He dead now."

Three fingers... Ah, yes—three generations. His great-grandfather, then. She was becoming quite used to Branko's peculiar way of communicating. "You mean your great-grandfather's home was there?"

"Great," he repeated, nodding. "Please, sit."

Heather was dying to ask more questions, but his limited vocabulary made that difficult. She sat down on a couch upholstered in an exquisite ecru damask. It suddenly struck her as odd that his home looked more like a European drawing room than the interior of a Romany caravan. From the little she'd learned about Gypsies, she knew that many of them didn't like to settle in one place and preferred bold vivid colors like red, yellow and purple.

On the rosewood coffee table she spied an ornate glass decanter and two cut-crystal glasses belonging to a set she could see in a curio cabinet next to the baby grand piano. Obviously Branko had been waiting for her. As soon as she was seated, he took out the glass stopper and poured a measure into each glass, then handed one to her.

Heather raised the glass and sniffed experimentally. She didn't drink hard liquor and had no idea what this was, but out of politeness decided to at least taste it. The sweet liquid burned its way down her throat and was so strong it brought tears to her eyes. She rested the nearly full glass on the table. Branko drank the contents of his in one swallow before eyeing her in his direct, bold way.

"I have gift for you."

She shook her head and told him, "You mustn't give me presents, Branko," but he didn't appear to be listening as he pulled something from his pants pocket.

Before she could anticipate his next move, he leaned over and quickly snapped a bracelet around her wrist. Like everything else about this house—and this Gypsy—the bracelet was unique. It looked as if it might have come from the treasury of some Eastern potentate. Five round rubylike gems set in gold were connected by tiny gold chains of the sheerest mesh. Heather gasped at the exquisite workmanship.

"Branko, you must know I can't accept this." She tried to take it off, but couldn't find the clasp.

"You not like?" he asked, his expression wounded. "In my tribe a husband give this to his wife before they marry. It belong to my *dej*. Before she die, she tell Branko to give to my woman. She bless it. That right? Bless?"

Ignoring his question, she looked down at the bracelet on her wrist, appalled he'd done such a thing. *This was the wedding gift from Branko's father to his mother!*

"Branko," she said sternly, "I can't possibly keep this and you know it. As your mother said, you must save it for the special woman in your life. Now please undo it!" she demanded. Enough was enough.

"*You* my woman," he said with dogged determination.

"No, I'm not!"

Branko's propensity for mischief had made her feel frustrated and impatient on several occasions. But this was the first time she'd ever been truly angry with him.

Right now she was in no mood to go along with his childish antics, and so was scarcely aware of a door slamming shut somewhere in the house.

"Now you not belong to anyone else." In a surprise move, he lifted her hand and kissed the palm fervently. As Heather stood there, stunned by the unexpected display of passion Jay had warned her about, a deep chilling male voice broke the unnatural silence.

"Now I know why the foreman at the sawmill traced me all the way to Bonner's Ferry. You were supposed to be at work by one, Branko—to finish what you didn't get done on Saturday. Would you like to tell me what's going on?"

CHAPTER TWO

HEATHER DIDN'T KNOW who was more shocked. She spun around guiltily, and Branko abruptly dropped her hand, flushing to the roots of his black hair.

A defensive volley of unintelligible Romany burst from his lips changing him into an intense fiery man she didn't recognize. Perhaps because he had the power of his own language to assist him, his behavior had undergone a disturbing change, bringing out what was clearly a more emotional side of his nature.

She shuddered as she recalled Jay's misgivings about her coming here alone. There was no Gypsy festival; that was obvious enough. Branko had lured her to his house under false pretenses. She bemoaned the fact that she was such a poor judge of character and, worse, had been caught in the cross fire of a private battle between this puzzling, lonely young man and his father.

"Speak English in front of your guest!" came the peremptory command. The man himself spoke with the slightest trace of an accent, and Heather stared at him. Despite the circumstances, she noticed what an arresting figure he made, wearing khakis and a navy sport shirt. He'd appeared in the entry without making a sound and stood there now, feet apart, hands thrust deep into his pockets.

"Ms. Martin, please meet my *dad*," Branko muttered. But whereas moments before he'd been carrying on with all the confidence of a man twice his age, his father's intimidating presence had reduced him to a belligerent teenager whose black eyes reflected anger ... and a glint of pain.

She looked across the room at Branko's father who by now had stepped inside. She could see he topped his son by several inches, and his build was leaner and more powerful. As far as she could tell, there wasn't a trace of Gypsy in him, which not only surprised her but made nonsense of all her preconceived notions about Branko's parentage.

"How do you do, Mr. Antonovic," she said. She would have extended her hand in greeting, but decided not to when he remained where he was and merely gave her an almost imperceptible nod of his head.

His skin was much lighter than Branko's, and he had strong features and slanted cheekbones. He wore his hair longer than Branko's, but it wasn't as dark or curly as his son's.

His eyes, wary and assessing, were the color of slate. They swept over her in one quick movement, clinically appraising her face and feminine attributes. The unusual contrast of her light hair and dark eyes, often made her the center of male attention, yet she'd never felt more exposed and vulnerable in her life.

Flicking his gaze to Branko, he said, "It's no longer a mystery why you rarely show up for the job on time

anymore. Obviously you've found a much more interesting way to entertain yourself in my absence."
Heather bristled at his words, and even more at his contemptuous tone. "I now have to ask myself how long this has been going on in my own home without my knowledge."

It took all her control to refrain from speaking up, because this was a private dispute between father and son. Unsettled as she was by Branko's deviousness, she still felt protective of him and sensed his humiliation. How had she been so blind when Jay had been able to see the real Branko in one evening?

Once more his father turned accusing eyes on Heather, and this time his scrutiny seemed vaguely threatening. A thrill of alarm ran through her body.

"I can't fault your taste, Branko. I dare say there aren't too many women who could compare to your *gadja*," he murmured, referring to her non-Gypsy status while subjecting her to another appraisal, more thorough than before. "It's your judgment I question. In the first place, she's too old for you—although that's a fascination I understand far better than you do," he added cryptically.

Anger robbed her of words and sent patches of color to her cheeks and throat. Branko hadn't been exaggerating when he said things weren't going well between him and his father. For one moment she felt a hysterical desire to fling the contents of her glass in his good-looking face and wipe the hateful mockery from his expression. How dared he treat Branko and her this way, no matter what he thought!

This situation was taking on all the qualities of a bad dream. Mesmerized, she watched the play of muscle beneath his shirt as he plucked the decanter from the table. "I wouldn't have minded your drinking anything else in the house. But *this*," he muttered, his black eyebrows slanting angrily, "I've been saving for many years, to be opened only for a very special occasion."

"This is special occasion. I drink with my woman, like you," Branko stated boldly.

A gasp escaped Heather's throat, not only at Branko's temerity in speaking to his father like that, but because of his amazing pronouncement. She could forgive him a lot of things he couldn't help; his indulging in a teenage fantasy, even if he'd taken it rather far, was to be expected. But equating his own adolescent dramatics with his father's private life put a totally different complexion on the matter.

"Yes, I can see that," his father said in a dangerously soft voice. "But I'm afraid you'll have to forgo your plans for the afternoon and say goodbye to—" he paused, casting her another hostile look "—Ms. Martin. I told Jack I'd track you down and make sure you got to work before the day was out."

He glanced at his watch. "If you leave now, you'll only have three hours to make up." Staring pointedly at Heather, he added, "I'm sure you'll understand. Please see her to the door, Branko," he ordered, putting the decanter away in the cabinet.

Heather was on the verge of making certain facts clear to him when Branko unexpectedly blurted, "She woman I marry!"

"Branko!" For once she was furious, completely and implacably furious with him. She grabbed hold of the couch arm to steady herself, reeling from the absurd declaration guaranteed to inflame his father. Until now she hadn't intervened because she wanted to spare Branko's feelings and intended to talk frankly to his father another time when they could be alone. But now Branko had gone too far and she turned to him, demanding he admit to his father that this was a joke. But he only shrugged and refused to speak.

"Mr. Antonovic..." she began. The words died on her lips as she saw his attention focus on the bracelet fastened on her wrist. She didn't imagine the sudden pallor of his complexion or the unnatural stillness that came over his body.

Cool hard eyes met hers for an interminable moment, as if he found her and the entire scenario distasteful. "You must have powers beyond comprehension to cause my son to part with his mother's marriage bracelet this soon in his young life."

"Marriage bracelet?" So Branko had been telling the truth. Her heart sank. She couldn't begin to understand all that was going on here, but one thing was unmistakable. Branko's father was outraged that his son had been foolish enough to give away a treasured family heirloom, and he wanted her to know it.

With a grimace he folded his arms on his broad chest. "Let's not pretend we don't know Branko has asked you to marry him. Obviously you accepted his proposal or you wouldn't be wearing the bracelet. That was your plan, wasn't it? To take advantage of his youth by using your beauty to maneuver yourself into this household?'' He shook his head. ''You've drunk the nuptial plum brandy. According to custom, the bracelet you wear is as binding as a wedding ring.''

Heather blinked in astonishment. ''I'm afraid there's been a misunderstanding. If we could talk privately for a moment?''

His eyes glittered like tiny ice shards. ''Considering you're such an intimate part of my son's life now, I can't see the point. Has Branko told you the bracelet you're wearing is priceless and constitutes his only earthly possession? It was bequeathed to him by his mother before she died.''

For at least a minute no one moved or said a word. Heather stared unseeingly at Branko's father while she assimilated everything. She could well believe he hated her for wearing the wedding jewelry he had given his wife, particularly since he was still in mourning.

Heather frowned at Branko and sought his gaze, expecting him to immediately retract his words, defusing a potentially explosive situation. But to her horror, he simply looked back at her with a satisfied gleam in his eyes. For reasons of his own, Branko had decided to show his father he wanted her for his wife, and in the Gypsy way had gone through the formalities.

What in heaven's name had possessed him to hurt his father this way—and to place her in such an ugly position?

The peaceful blue lake she could see beyond his shoulder seemed to mock her inner turmoil. She had read somewhere that Gypsies practiced endogamy, never marrying outside the tribe. Parents sometimes spent up to a hundred thousand dollars to buy wives for their sons. Branko had apparently taken it upon himself to do the honors, but in this case he'd offered for a *gadja*. Was that the other reason his father was so angry? Because Heather wasn't a Gypsy? She couldn't fathom any of it, but intended to put an end to this confusion right now!

"Mr. Antonovic," she said determinedly, "since your—"

But she didn't get the rest of her words out because he cut her off. "It obviously hasn't escaped your notice that Branko depends totally on me for his support. He doesn't have the means to take care of himself, let alone anyone else, at this point. If you have some idea that once you're married you can move in here with my son so I'll provide for both of you, then you're sadly mistaken."

His remarks hit a nerve. What if she'd really been in love with Branko and had wanted to be introduced to his father as his fiancée? What was wrong with him that he could treat them in such a cold ruthless fashion, without even a word of explanation? No doubt he was in pain over his wife's death, but that didn't excuse his insensitivity toward his son—a son who was still suffering the loss of his mother.

Her brown eyes flashed her disdain, and right then Heather would have loved nothing more than to tell him what she thought of his attitude. But she couldn't lose control in front of Branko. "I wouldn't dream of keeping the bracelet or moving in here with you, Mr. Antonovic."

His lips broke into a wintry smile. "I thought maybe you'd change your mind when you found out the two of you would have to make it on your own."

The man was impossible. He acted as though she was some kind of opportunist who'd taken advantage of his Gypsy son. For what reason? To inherit his father's money? Was he so wealthy? Except to make an occasional derogatory comment, Branko had never discussed his father with her.

On the verge of hysteria, she turned to Branko and extended her arm. "Please take it off. You know I can't keep it."

Branko shook his dark curly head. "You my woman now."

This was a nightmare, but she thought at least she understood Branko's infatuation. His feelings were all mixed up with the death of his mother and his need for the companionship he hadn't found with his father. "You're a fine young man, Branko, and some day you're going to find the right woman for you." She tried to speak calmly. "But I'm not that person. I can't be."

"You woman I marry," he insisted, and she thought she detected tears. But she'd been moved by them once before and now knew she didn't trust them.

"Branko..." she prompted him, but he purposely avoided her gaze and looked out the picture window so that Heather couldn't see his expression, twirling his fedora between his hands. "What your father said was true. Aside from all the other reasons marriage isn't possible, I'm too old for you, and you're too young for me.''

At first she thought she'd gotten through to him because he was so quiet. But then he wheeled around, training narrowed black eyes on his father. The hate she saw there sent a shiver of fear through her body.

Suddenly there was an explosion of sound as Branko said something in Romany and his father answered in kind. Heather didn't need a translator to realize the two men had reached a total impasse. But not even she was prepared for the resounding slap Branko administered to his father's cheek before he shoved him out of the way with both hands and left the house on a run.

''Branko!'' she cried out, aghast. But he'd moved with lightning speed, and by the time she reached the front porch, he'd started up the Jeep and driven off.

Heather stood there clinging to the porch rail. Not in her wildest dreams had she imagined him capable of that kind of violence. Because of his vulnerability, she had always made excuses for him. But this time she couldn't possibly justify his behavior. No matter how much pain Branko or his father were feeling, she couldn't dismiss the cruelty they'd shown toward each other.

Feeling distinctly ill because she'd been the reason for their latest domestic crisis, she ran down the steps and hurried to her Wagoneer, anxious to get as far away as possible. She needed a chance to put everything into perspective, to come up with a strategy for dealing with this confused and unhappy young man.

But she hadn't realized Branko's father had followed her outside. When she tried to start the engine, he reached through the open window and placed one firm hand over hers, applying enough pressure to prevent her from turning the key.

"How dare you!" She flung her head around, but that action only served to bring her face closer to his.

"I dare because Branko needs time alone to cool off and think things through. That would be impossible with you around." *He actually believed she was going after Branko!* For the space of a heartbeat she thought she detected a haunted look in his eyes. But when she saw the set of his taut mouth, she decided she'd been mistaken.

To Heather's embarrassment, a warm breeze caused tendrils of her hair to brush against his cheek, where she could still see the red imprint of Branko's hand. That slap must have hurt, she acknowledged, though deep in her heart she felt he deserved it.

Through gritted teeth she muttered, "As long as I'm being detained, would you please remove the bracelet? I can't seem to find the clasp." Without looking at him, she held out her arm, praying to be relieved of the jewelry that had adorned his wife's wrist. It had become a hateful symbol of this terrible, distressing day, and right now her control was on the verge of snapping.

"It's a little late to try impressing me with your good intentions when we both know you've manipulated a naïve young man to your own advantage. I'm sure he's told you those authentic Burmese rubies are worth a small fortune. Branko gave you his mother's bracelet, Ms. Martin. It's yours now to do with as you please." After a brief pause he added, "I have no doubt you will."

Shaken with outrage by his false assumptions, she couldn't speak. But when she tried to start the van, wanting only to escape, he trapped her hand once more. "Let's give Branko a head start, shall we?"

Angrily she yanked the keys from the ignition to avoid his touch. However, he'd braced himself against the door, making it impossible for her to ignore his proximity.

"While we're waiting, why don't you tell me where you come from, how you met my son in the first place and how long you've been carrying on an affair in my home. Let's start with the fact that you're driving a car bearing Washington license plates."

She lifted her chin defiantly. "It's a little late in the day to be asking me questions. If I were you, I'd be much more concerned about your son. Though I could never condone striking another person, I have to admit he had plenty of provocation. You're the most pathetic, despicable excuse for a father I've ever met!"

Though he didn't move, she noted a tightening of his face that should have warned her to stop. But things had gone too far, and she could no longer hold back her disgust. "When your son told me he was unhappy living with you, I thought it was nothing more than the typical teenage complaint. But after seeing you in action, I'm surprised he hasn't run away long before now!"

He flashed her a furious glance. "Since it's probably safe to say you're not a parent, I think we'll pass on your opinion."

She flinched at the remark, still finding it difficult to accept the fact that she'd never have a child of her own. "Although I'm not a parent, I *am* Branko's ESL teacher and I believe that qualifies me to speak with some authority on the subject of your son."

He burst out in an angry laugh. "You'll have to do better than that, because I happen to know a Mrs. Wood is his teacher."

She tossed her head. "Mrs. Wood resigned after Thanksgiving to take care of her sick husband. I'm Heather Martin, an ESL teacher from Spokane," she explained, relishing the moment. "I was called in to fill the vacancy until a permanent teacher could be found. Any meetings I've had with your son have been in the spirit of friendship and academic pursuit only!"

"Whether that's true or not," he muttered, all expression suddenly wiped from his face, "I must remind you that my son could find himself in serious trouble if he *has* run away."

She frowned, drumming her fingers against the steering wheel. Was it possible that Branko had never told his father about the change in teachers? After today she realized the boy was capable of just about anything. But why had he kept it a secret? And where could he possibly have gone?

After a sustained pause she heard him say, "Branko never mentioned anything about a new teacher to me."

"Did you give him the chance?" she fired back, warming to her subject. "Since when do you do anything for your son except issue orders? If he needed a little tenderness or a quiet moment of sharing to discuss his crush on a teacher, it would only fall on deaf ears, as I witnessed today."

A tiny nerve leapt at the corner of his mouth. "I think you've said enough."

"I haven't even begun!"

At her reckless words, his hands tightened into fists and he straightened to his full height. She took advantage of the freedom to jam her key in the ignition and start the engine.

Once it was idling, she glared at him over her shoulder. "Do you know what disturbs me most, Mr. Antonovic? For the past six months Branko's been the top student in my ESL class. But after today, I'll be surprised if he ever shows his face again. And that's something your conscience will have to live with. For what it's worth, the community school in Spokane offers a night class in parenting. *You* should sign up, if it isn't too late!

"And don't worry," she supplied as an afterthought. "Though my teacher's salary can't possibly compare to your wealth, I'll refrain from the temptation of selling off the rubies, and send the bracelet back to you intact!"

"We'll see," he muttered enigmatically, and in her fury she threw the van into drive and stamped down hard on the accelerator. She left him standing in an eddy of swirling pine needles and screeched down the private drive.

She headed for Spokane with her emotions seething. She couldn't imagine how either Branko or his father would be able to mend the breach between them now. And at the moment she was too resentful of Branko for placing her in this position to imagine remaining his friend. As for his father, she prayed she'd never have anything to do with him again. Then her thoughts returned to Branko. Genuine fear for the boy—he was young, naïve, reckless—started to creep into her fury.

Her black mood lasted all the way back to Spokane, and she pulled into the garage a little before seven. Jay's car was still parked in front of the house. She hurried inside but couldn't find a soul. Where was everybody?

When she walked out onto the patio, which overlooked the river, the domestic tranquility that greeted her was such a far cry from the emotional scene at the Antonovics she wondered if the past few hours had been a bad dream, after all.

Her mother and Shelley had been playing with the baby on an afghan spread beneath a large maple tree, and all three had fallen asleep. Her father lay sprawled in the hammock, out for the count. Only Jay hadn't succumbed to the languor of the warm June evening; he was absorbed in a golf magazine. He looked up when he saw her.

His brows lifted in silent query as she motioned for him to follow her into the study, which served as a repository for pictures, plaques and the hundred or so trophies Heather and Jay had won. "So, how did it go?" he asked when they were alone. "You're back a lot sooner than I expected."

"*This* is how it went." She lifted her arm to display the bracelet.

Jay chuckled. "You've never walked away from a carnival in your life without bringing home an armload of junk. Let me have a look."

His eyes narrowed as he fingered the fine gold teeth and held the red jewels to the light. A low whistle escaped his lips. "It actually looks real. How much did you pay for it?"

She swallowed hard. "I'm afraid I'm in a lot deeper than you could possibly imagine."

"Hez?"

"I'll explain everything in a minute, but first I'd like you to do me a favor and take it off. I don't know how to undo the clasp."

Jay glanced at her as if she'd lost her mind, but set about the task with total concentration. One minute stretched into two, then three. He swore softly beneath his breath and turned the bracelet around experimenting this way and that, trying without success to find the catch. "Do you remember how it fastened in the first place?"

Heather took a deep breath. "I haven't the faintest idea. Branko put it on me."

"You didn't buy it?"

"No."

Their gazes locked, and streams of unspoken words passed between them.

"What did Branko do, buy *you?*" he teased with an infectious grin. But his smile slowly faded when she didn't laugh with him. "I had a feeling that guy was up to something," he muttered. "What happened?"

CHAPTER THREE

AT TEN THE NEXT MORNING, Heather sat perched on a stool in front of a display case at Leyson's while the head jeweler used his loupe to examine the bracelet on her wrist.

Normally she would have been at school on a Monday morning. But after a discussion with her family the night before, she'd decided that the only way to remove the bracelet was to consult an expert. So she'd called for a substitute to teach her classes and took the rest of the day off to solve her dilemma.

For half an hour or more she watched Mr. Beacom try to locate the clasp from every conceivable angle. Finally he shook his gray head in defeat.

"How did you say you came by this?"

"A Gypsy gave it to me, but I can't accept it and need to return it to him as soon as possible."

"Ah, that might explain the secret catch. Whoever he is must care for you very much. Are you aware it's worth a small fortune?"

At this point nothing surprised her. It seemed Branko's father hadn't exaggerated about anything. "I was told the rubies are real."

He nodded. "It reminds me of an ancient marriage choker from India I once saw at the Victoria and Albert Museum in London. The rubies alone could bring fifty to sixty thousand dollars on today's market.''

"That much?'' She gasped in astonishment. No wonder Mr. Antonovic had been suspicious of her interest in his son. Because it was a family heirloom, she was surprised he'd allowed her to drive off without demanding some kind of collateral.

But he must have realized at some point that she was telling the truth about being Branko's teacher and knew he could track her down if necessary. If Mr. Antonovic was a wealthy man, as he'd implied, his interest in recovering the bracelet would have more to do with sentiment than money.

"The stones may have come from an original piece found incomplete, so a copy was made,'' Mr. Beacom said "Perhaps it was a Gypsy who asked the artisan to fashion the hidden clasp.''

"All I really care about is getting it off and returning it to the owner. Unfortunately he's not…available just now.'' And she had no idea when he would be. That did worry her. But it worried her even more, at this point, to find herself responsible for anything so valuable. The fact that no one could steal it from her arm was small consolation.

Suddenly Mr. Antonovic's parting comment, "We'll see,'' when she said she'd send the bracelet back to him intact, made sense. He knew all about the secret catch! Heather's anger kindled again, but she had to contain it in front of Mr. Beacom.

"Well, it could be taken apart, but that would lower the value irreparably. I hesitate to damage it.''

"No, I don't want it damaged,'' she said slowly.

"My advice is to get hold of your Gypsy friend and ask him to unfasten it."

That was obviously the most logical course, but if Branko didn't show up for class on Tuesday night, what would she do? How long would it be before she saw him again? More concerned and frustrated than ever, she slid off the stool. "I don't really have a choice except to take your advice. Thank you for your time, Mr. Beacom. I appreciate it."

"I wish I could have helped you. Let me know the outcome. I'm extremely curious to find out how it works."

"So am I. I'll drop by one day and tell you," she said with more optimism than she felt. When she was halfway out the door, he called to her.

"Yes?" She paused in the entry and turned toward him.

"It's just a thought, but perhaps you could consult some other Gypsies in the area. It seems to me I've seen a tearoom in the downtown area. Perhaps one of them could be persuaded to reveal how the bracelet works."

Why didn't I think of that? Bestowing a warm smile on him, she said, "What a wonderful idea! I know exactly where it is. Thank you."

"Well, on the outside chance that both plans fail, let me know and I'll phone a colleague in New York who can put us on to an expert."

"Thanks, Mr. Beacom. But I hope it doesn't come to that."

Fifteen minutes later, Heather parked in the back lot of her father's fabric store and went inside to discuss the idea with him. Unfortunately he'd just left for a meeting with the manager at his outlet on East Sprague. Then she tried reaching Jay at his office, but he was in court. Since her mother had gone shopping with Shelley, there was no one to consult about the wisdom of asking the Gypsies for help.

But she was feeling desperate. Who knew when Branko would appear at the school in Priest River again? There were no guarantees he'd ever come back to class. When she rejected him in front of his father, she'd inflicted a serious blow to his pride. Instinctively she knew it would take Branko a long time to forgive either of them.

What could it hurt to simply ask the Gypsies if they knew how to undo the bracelet? The more she thought about it, the more it made sense. And even if the giving of a marriage bracelet was an obscure practice among the Romany, surely some of the Gypsies had heard of it and could refer her to a person who might help.

Deciding she'd better go prepared, Heather wrote a check for fifty dollars and asked the assistant manager to cash it. She also told the older woman where she was going, in case her father returned early and wanted to join her. Then she left the store and headed for the tearoom, which had been closed on Saturday.

Today, however, she was in luck. The bright yellow curtains with black tassels were pulled back framing the Open sign in the window.

Heather hadn't known what to expect, but was slightly disappointed when she opened the door and found herself inside what looked like a doctor's waiting room. The small area was carpeted in a burnt-orange shag and contained several chairs and an end table facing the counter. The unadorned walls were painted the same shade of yellow as the curtains. A handmade sign hanging on the wall said Palms read by Zamura—$25.

Heather had to smile, remembering her childhood. To think after all the years of passing the tearoom and imagining something exotic and wonderful behind those curtains, she'd finally discover anything as ordinary as this reception room.

She could hear voices from the draped alcove behind the counter, and a few moments later one of the young Gypsy women she'd seen in her father's store came out front with two small children in tow. A spark of recognition illuminated her black eyes as they rested on Heather.

The Gypsy woman was heavily made up, yet couldn't be much older than Heather. A little over five feet tall and fashionably thin, she wore a flowered print blouse in bright colors with a long purple skirt. She was bedecked with rings on her fingers, bracelets on her arms and several necklaces at her throat. Long silver earrings dangled from her ears amidst a profusion of black curly hair. Heather thought she was quite beautiful and felt drab by comparison in her beige shirtwaist dress.

"You want your palm read?" the woman asked without preamble. Though she had an accent, it wasn't nearly as heavy as Branko's.

"Are you Zamura?" Heather asked, deciding not to explain the purpose of her visit until she'd met the Gypsy in charge of the tearoom.

"No. I'll tell her you're here."

"Thank you." Heather took a seat, hoping this Zamura could help her. She supported her wrist, chafing it gently. Apart from all the other reasons she didn't want to be wearing Branko's bracelet, she was unaccustomed to the weight of it. From an early age she'd spent so much time in and out of the water, first at swim meets and then at waterskiing competitions, she'd gotten in the habit of leaving her jewelry at home.

It felt strange to have something shackled to her wrist. When she'd showered that morning, she'd taken care not to get it wet. But many more days of the metal constantly rubbing against her skin could prove irritating.

Did Branko's mother actually wear this bracelet all her life, the way some women wore wedding rings? Did she never take it off? Did she occasionally feel trapped at being bound like this? Or had she loved her husband so much that—

"Zamura says you may come back now."

Heather welcomed the intrusion of the Gypsy's voice since she didn't particularly like her own train of thought. She got up from the chair and followed the other woman around the back of the counter and through the curtain to a smaller, windowless room.

An old Gypsy woman resembling Heather's idea of a fortune-teller in her blood-red satin blouse, black vest and skirt, sat before a square wooden table. Except for a lighted floor lamp and folding chair, the room was devoid of adornment. There was a door situated directly behind the woman, which probably led to the family apartment.

The two Gypsies looked surprisingly alike, which suggested they were related, but the disparity in years probably put Zamura in the grandmother category.

"Come closer." She waved an arthritic-looking hand heavy with rings and bracelets of every description. The woman had to be in her late seventies, yet her wavy black shoulder-length hair showed no signs of graying.

A prominent Roman nose kept her from being truly beautiful, but she had an arresting face and jet-black eyes that reminded Heather of Branko. However, where he was tall and well-built like his father, she and the younger Gypsy were small in stature and probably came from a country other than Yugoslavia.

"Have you ever had your palm read before?" the woman asked in heavily accented English while Heather sat down in the vacant chair. It put the two women at eye level.

"No. Actually, I'm not here for a palm reading. I was hoping you might be able to help me with a problem."

The Gypsy gazed at her and blinked several times. "You wish me to study the tea leaves or see what the Tarot cards have to say? Perhaps you want me to gaze into my crystal ball or make contact with a loved one on the other side? I can accommodate you."

Heather fought the urge to smile. The woman before her was the personification of every hokey carnival fortune-teller she'd ever seen. Still, if Zamura knew the secret of the clasp, Heather's visit was worth it.

"No. I'm here for another reason altogether. What I'd like you to do is tell me if you know how to undo the clasp on *this*." She unfastened the cuff of her sleeve at the wrist and rolled it back to expose the bracelet. "It was given to me by someone of the Rom."

Heather heard a gasp as Zamura sat up in the chair and placed both hands palm down on the table. Gone was the old woman's complacency. "May I see it please?" Her voice actually shook as she asked the question, her avid eyes never straying from the bracelet.

Encouraged by the Gypsy's spontaneous reaction, Heather stretched out her right hand. The old woman's head bent low over the bracelet, but she didn't touch it, or Heather's hand. All the while she made strange sounds and muttered Romany words beneath her breath. She kept repeating the words *baro manursh,* until Heather asked her what they meant. But the Gypsy seemed to have gone into some kind of trance and didn't answer.

Anxious to get this over with, Heather said, "Do you know how the catch works? Can you undo the bracelet for me? I'll pay you double what you charge for a palm reading."

The old Gypsy lifted her head and glared angrily at Heather. "You are a *gadja*. What can you expect?" She waved her hands dismissively as if to emphasize her low opinion of Heather's non-Gypsy status. "Zamura does not interfere with the signs. To do so would bring bad luck, even death.''

Heather couldn't believe the Gypsy wouldn't undo the bracelet, even to earn fifty dollars. Maybe the woman felt insulted to be offered so little for doing something that required a Gypsy's services. ''I'll tell you what. If you'll agree to take off the bracelet, I'll go to the bank and bring you back a hundred dollars in cash.''

But it was the wrong thing to say because the old woman's expression grew fierce. ''Foolish *gadja*. You understand nothing!''

Zamura was turning out to be as stubborn as Branko. ''Then can you tell *me* how to undo it?'' Heather asked, feeling somewhat desperate at this point.

''I cannot!'' Zamura sat back in her chair with her hands clasped beneath her bosom. ''Once it goes on, it travels with you through life.''

''Madame Zamura,'' Heather beseeched her, ''a Gypsy named Branko Antonovic gave it to me. His father's name is Nick. Do you know them?''

''I do not. And if I did, it would make no difference.''

Heather could see it was futile to try to persuade the woman to change her mind. Since nothing could be accomplished here, she reached for her handbag and pulled twenty-five dollars from her wallet. ''This is to thank you for your time.''

The Gypsy made no move to take the bills. ''Put it away, *gadja*. Zamura does not take money from a *hanamika*.''

Hanamika was another word Branko had taught Heather. It meant "friend" in Romany. "But we've never met before today!"

The old woman made a clicking sound with her tongue. "You wear ruby bracelet. That makes you *hanamika*." Though Heather couldn't take any of this seriously, she allowed Zamura to finish her spiel. "May I look at your other hand, please?"

Heather nodded. She had never inspected her palms this closely before, but when the Gypsy pointed them out, she could see four definite lines running parallel at the juncture of her hand and lower arm.

"These four lines are called the royal bracelet. Do you notice how they match the mesh chains of the ruby bracelet, which are braided into four gold cords encircling your other wrist?"

"Yes?"

"It means you have the double sign." The old woman began talking faster and faster, as if there was too much to say and not enough time to say it. "Ah," she muttered. "A great man has come into your life. A stranger. He will have great influence over you, and together you will gain all the world has to offer."

This time Heather did smile. She couldn't help remembering a school carnival years before. Everyone's fortune was the same. "You will meet a tall dark stranger and take a long journey."

She could have told the Gypsy that Branko's father was the only stranger she'd met. But he was the antithesis of what she considered a great man! Just remembering their final exchange brought a wave of heat to her face.

The Gypsy's eyes narrowed. "I see you don't believe me, but the rubies do not lie. This man will bring you fortune and happiness and take away your sorrow."

Though she couldn't possibly put any stock in the Gypsy's words, Heather was surprised the woman had mentioned sorrow.

"You think Zamura is a fool, but it is all written there in your hand. You have suffered a serious illness, which has brought you pain. But with the help of the great man, you will live to an old age and enjoy health, wealth and love."

Deciding she'd had enough, Heather started to get up, but the Gypsy detained her by clutching her. "You don't believe me, but I will tell you one last thing. This man will be the only great love of your life."

To Heather's irritation, the image of Branko's autocratic father passed through her mind once more. The notion that *he* could ever become her one great love was so absurd, a slight groan rose in her throat.

"That's all very interesting," she murmured politely. But just now she didn't think she wanted to hear any more and pulled her hand away. "Thank you for the reading, Madame Zamura." She got up from the chair, deliberately leaving the twenty-five dollars on the table.

"Take your money with you, *gadja.* I cannot touch it. It will bring me bad luck. Before you go, Zamura must tell you one more thing."

"Yes?"

"There is a star on the mound below your thumb. This means trouble in love."

Heather's first instinct was to roll her eyes, but she managed to remain poker-faced. "I thought you said there'd only be one great love in my life and we'd be happy."

The old woman pressed her palms together and touched her forehead. "First must come the rain, then the rainbow."

After saying goodbye, Heather walked through the curtain to the reception room. A young couple was talking to the pretty Gypsy about having their palms read by Zamura. They were holding hands and whispering to each other, hardly aware of their surroundings.

Heather stood there for a moment, thinking Zamura had made a mistake. She should have given Heather's fortune to the happy lovers. At least that way there was a possibility that some of it might come true.

She chatted with the young Gypsy for a few minutes, then waved to the two black-eyed toddlers clinging to their mother's skirt and left the tearoom. Not wanting to think about anything the old Gypsy had said, she hurried to her father's store in the hope that she could talk to him about the bracelet. Not surprisingly, he hadn't returned from his meeting.

Needing advice, she called Jay's office and was relieved to find him back. He agreed to meet her at the delicatessen around the corner from his firm.

"How did it go?" he asked as she slipped into the booth opposite him ten minutes later. He'd ordered pastrami for both of them and had a bottle of chilled grape juice waiting for Heather. She took a long swal-

low before rolling up her sleeve to display the bracelet.

"As you can see, it's still with me."

Jay stopped munching on his sandwich. "Why
didn't you have the jeweler cut it off?"

"I planned to, until he told me the rubies alone were
worth fifty or sixty thousand dollars."

"You're joking!"

Heather smoothed the blond hair away from her
temples. "I wish I were. That's why I wanted to have
lunch with you or Dad to discuss the idea of getting it
insured. I'd hate for anything to happen to it. Apparently it's very similar to an ancient wedding choker
from India, and Mr. Beacom said it would devalue the
bracelet to touch it. I can't take that chance."

"Under the circumstances, I agree with you."
Shaking his head, he groaned loudly. "That Branko
Antonovic has turned out to be a bundle of trouble."

She took a deep breath. "What Branko did was
wrong, but you can't blame him for caring about me.
His actions don't make him a criminal. I seem to recall you had a serious crush on your math teacher back
in high school."

"That was different."

"No, it wasn't. You used to hang around every day
after school so you could give her a ride to the bus stop
on your motorcycle. Everybody knew how you felt."

He stopped eating and gave her his famous courtroom scowl. "Well, I sure as hell didn't put a shackle
on her arm."

Heather burst out laughing. "Are you trying to tell me you wouldn't have if you could've? Because if you are, I don't believe you."

After a second she heard him laugh in self-mockery. "All right. Point taken. Maybe he's already regretting what he's done by now and will show up for class tomorrow night. Because it was his mother's, he'd have to be aware of the bracelet's value."

Heather looked down at her plate, but couldn't muster the appetite to finish her sandwich. "If I've learned anything since Saturday afternoon, it's that Branko didn't behave impulsively. On the contrary, he worked hard to win my trust over six long months before he made his move. And when he did, he had everything figured out down to the last detail. The only unknown was his father, who showed up unexpectedly. Between the two of us, we pretty well destroyed Branko's fantasy. Which is why I don't think he'll be there tomorrow night."

Jay put the money for their meal on the table. "He'll get over it one day. I speak from personal experience." He winked. "The point is, can you stand to wear the bracelet for as long as it takes Branko to come around?"

"Then you finally agree with me—Branko's just a mixed-up teenager."

"I didn't say that exactly."

"Jay..."

"I'll concede he probably has an outsized crush on you. You're quite something, you know, even if you are my little sister."

"Don't you see? His feelings are all mixed up because of the mother he lost. Can you imagine living a tribal life as a Gypsy, only to be uprooted from your country to come here? He's lonely, Jay, and needs someone to love him."

"He has a father."

She sucked in her breath. "If they were handing out prizes for the world's worst parent, he'd win it hands down."

"Hez, that doesn't sound like you. Aren't those pretty strong words when you've only met the man once? You have to admit that what Branko did would try any father's patience, especially one who's still mourning his wife's death."

"It was more than that, Jay. He was so cold and remote. Enough to make me realize why Branko's been so desperate for affection." Suddenly Heather could read Jay's mind. "I know what you're thinking. Since I was told I couldn't have children, I've gone all maternal over Branko."

"Have you?"

"Maybe. But not consciously. Even so, it doesn't excuse Nick Antonovic's offensive behavior. He jumped to conclusions and had both of us drawn and quartered, as Daddy loves to say, without knowing any of the facts. What bothers me is that he didn't *want* to hear any explanations. It was as if he took one look at us and something snapped.

"I've never been through an experience like it. And to think poor Branko has to live with the man! Part of me would cheer if Branko never darkened his father's door again. After witnessing the way he struck him, I can't believe they're good for each other."

Jay eyed her speculatively. "You don't really mean that, Hez. According to what you told the folks, it was a miracle his father didn't strike back. Tell me more about this Nick Antonovic."

"I don't want to discuss him. In fact, if I never see him again, it'll be too soon."

"You told me you don't think he's a Gypsy. If that's true, has it occurred to you Branko might be adopted?"

Heather shook her head. "Branko's his natural son," she said firmly. "The man has the same build, only...only more so...." Her voice trailed as another picture of Branko's father came to mind. "Well, you've met Branko, so you know what I mean."

"Yeah. If Shelley's reaction is anything to go by." He grinned. "So, is he old? Young? What does he do for a living?"

"I haven't the faintest idea how he makes his money, but he must make a considerable amount judging by what he said and where he lives. As for his age, he'd have to be in his mid-thirties at least to have fathered Branko. But since I don't think he ever passed through that period known as the precarious teenage years, I'd place him closer to fifty."

"As old as that," Jay interjected smoothly.

Heather blinked. "Are you putting me on?" When Jay laughed, she laughed, too. "You are! You beast!"

"I couldn't resist. You've never gone on about a man like this in your whole life!"

"Maybe that's because there could only be one like him per millenium!" On that note, she got up from the table, suddenly feeling uncomfortably warm and out of sorts.

"Now you've got me curious," he said, rising to his feet. "I wish I didn't have to take a deposition this afternoon so we could continue this fascinating discussion."

"There's nothing remotely fascinating about Mr. Antonovic, Jay."

"You've never been a good liar. I can see all the signs."

"Now you're beginning to sound like Madame Zamura."

"Who's that?"

"The Gypsy fortune-teller at the tearoom down the street from Dad's store. Mr. Beacom thought maybe she'd know how to remove the bracelet."

"And you went there?" He laughed again.

"I know. It was a dumb idea."

"How much did she charge you?"

"She didn't. In fact, she read my palm for free."

"And I bet she told you you were going to meet a tall dark stranger!" His grin was contagious.

"Actually, she told me I'd already met him."

"Well, that was easy enough for a five-year-old to figure out."

"Except she said he was a great man." Again her mind conjured up Branko's father....

"Well, she would, wouldn't she?" Jay chuckled. "Since that bracelet's worth a small fortune, naturally she'd think the donor was Santa Claus himself. It's economics, Hez."

"I know. She also told me I'd suffered from a serious illness."

"Of course. Anyone approaching thirty has probably suffered from a serious health problem at one time or other."

"Oh, let's not talk about it anymore. Do you know a good insurance agent for something like this?"

"I do. Fred Morton in the Kibbe building. Tell him I referred you."

"Thanks, Jay."

"You're welcome. How about pulling me skiing tonight after work?"

"How about you pulling me?"

"You're on. Shelley and I'll be over at six. Make sure you have an extra life-preserver handy."

"Don't you think Stacy's a little young to get up on skis?"

"I was thinking about your safety. With that bracelet on, you might just sink to the bottom of the river."

"That isn't funny, Jay."

CHAPTER FOUR

HEATHER ARRIVED at Priest River an hour early for her Tuesday-night class, in the faint hope that Branko would be waiting for her. In any case she needed the extra time to catch up on paperwork. And if Branko did come, they'd be able to talk without anyone else around. But of course he didn't show up. At least, she'd taken steps to insure the bracelet.

One of her worries now was that Branko would be conspicuous by his absence. She didn't want the others asking questions and perhaps making things more awkward for him, if and when he did return. He'd never missed class before, so everyone would speculate on what had happened to him.

Mr. Cheng didn't come, either. Heather's Laotian student had left word with the office that he wouldn't be able to attend because his wife had had a baby. But he'd be there on Thursday.

Throughout the evening session, which seemed to go on endlessly, Heather kept wishing the door would open and Branko would slip in. By eight-thirty her spirits had reached an all-time low, and she decided she'd better do something about her depressed state of mind or it would affect her students. At quarter to nine she told them to stop working because she had an announcement to make.

"As you know, Mrs. Cheng has just had a baby boy. I think it would be nice if we gave Mr. Cheng a surprise baby shower on Thursday night. We can bring food and some presents for the baby."

At first everyone was silent until she explained what a baby shower was. Then they got excited and, because of the great camaraderie that existed, organized the party in no time at all. Heather offered to make decorations and bring the punch. She urged the others to stay within their budgets, aware that most of them struggled to make ends meet.

One by one they handed her their work and said good-night, obviously excited about the forthcoming event. She prayed Branko would show up on Thursday night, pleasantly surprised when he discovered a party in progress.

As soon as the last student had gone out the door, Heather erased the blackboard and started putting papers away in her briefcase, all the while worrying about Branko. She had a strong urge to call his home to see if he was there. But the mere thought of having to deal with his obdurate father caused her to reject the idea.

"Ms. Martin? If I could have a word with you?"

Heather jumped at the sound of the one voice she hoped never to hear again and lifted her head to gaze across the room at Branko's father. It was as if just thinking about him had conjured him up. She decided the term "tall dark stranger" could have been coined with him in mind. He wore a black silk shirt and hip-hugging jeans and moved with a casual grace she'd rarely observed in a man. She tried not to stare at the way the material clung to his powerful thighs as he drew near.

"Good evening, Mr. Antonovic." Her role as a teacher dictated she be civil, but if he expected anything more from her, he was going to be unpleasantly surprised. She saw the way his eyes narrowed as he glanced at the bracelet on her wrist. Obviously he couldn't believe she was still wearing it. Her chin lifted in silent challenge.

He stood in front of her desk with his legs slightly apart, his arms folded. This close she could tell he hadn't been sleeping well. Either that, or he'd been ill. His tanned skin had an underlying pallor that made his slightly disheveled hair look darker than ever. And she noticed deep grooves around his mouth, which gave him an almost gaunt appearance.

The change in him since Sunday was quite dramatic, disturbingly so, and Heather was amazed that she could still find his appearance attractive and even compelling. She suddenly remembered Branko's sly reference to another woman....

Unfathomable gray eyes searched hers for a long moment. "I think you know why I'm here, Ms. Martin. It's vital I find Branko, and I have the feeling you know where he is."

No one in her life had ever made her as furious as Branko's father. Yet, coupled with her rage was a growing anxiety over Branko's disappearance. The careless comments she'd made to Jay came back to haunt her.

It was no mystery why Branko's father looked worried. Though he deserved to suffer after the way he'd treated his son, the fact remained that Branko was no ordinary runaway. An immigrant on the loose without the proper identification papers could be in serious trouble with the law. Despite herself, Heather felt a surge of compassion for Nick Antonovic. The loss of his wife and now the estrangement from his son must be terribly difficult.

"You may have difficulty believing this, Mr. Antonovic, but I haven't the faintest idea where Branko is."

His mouth thinned into a taut line. "Surely you don't expect me to buy that. Even if he had no intentions of attending class, at some point he would have made contact with you."

Anger over his continued false assumptions about her relationship with Branko brought color flaming to her cheeks. "After what happened on Sunday, I don't know how you could think Branko would want to see or talk to either one of us!"

There was a long pause while he appeared to absorb what she'd said. "If you're about to remind me again what a terrible job I've done as a father, you won't be saying anything I haven't said to myself hundreds of times since I brought Branko here from Yugoslavia," he muttered, his voice dull and expressionless.

She blinked in astonishment. But even she was surprised when she said, "Your wife's death must have been very painful for both you and Branko. It couldn't be easy raising him alone, especially in a strange country."

An uncomfortable silence followed her comments, making Heather wish she hadn't said anything of a personal nature.

"Contrary to what Branko may have told you, I never married his Gypsy mother."

It was astonishing how one new piece of information could wipe out months of conjecture.

She held on to the back of the chair to steady herself. "Perhaps not in the traditional way. Branko has told me the Rom functions by its own set of rules and standards."

His eyes darkened. "You don't seem to understand, Ms. Martin. Branko's mother and I were never married according to *any* tradition!"

Perhaps there had been no formal ceremony, but Heather felt quite sure the marriage bracelet meant this man's commitment to his dead lover was more binding than any piece of paper. For some nebulous reason, the knowledge disturbed Heather, and she forced her thoughts to dwell on Branko, who might conceivably be upset by his parents' unmarried status. It could explain some of his pain.

"I had no idea," she offered in a controlled voice. "Branko only said his mother and great-grandfather were dead. And he'd never mentioned either fact before last Sunday. Certainly he's never shared any details with me. Even if he understands nearly everything said to him, he can't converse fluently. But...but of course you don't need me to tell you about your son."

"I think you did a fairly complete job of that on Sunday," he retorted bitterly. "In only six months you've managed to establish a rapport with him—

something that hasn't happened with anyone else. Including me. He not only picked you for his woman, he felt comfortable enough to confide in you about me."

His comments reminded her of their hostile conversation in front of his house, and a wave of heat washed over her. No matter how justified she'd felt at the time, it was disconcerting to recall how she'd attacked his fathering skills.

Bristling at his obvious dislike of her, she said, "All teenagers need an outlet, Mr. Antonovic. In that regard, Branko's no different from anyone else his age. That, plus the recent loss of his mother, would explain his attachment to me."

"Let's not play games, Ms. Martin," he snapped. "My son is crazy about you. I doubt very much that there's anything filial about his fantasies. An eighteen-year-old can have the wants and needs of a man in his prime. Perhaps he even feels them more strongly because he hasn't learned to bridle his passions."

Her hands curled at her sides. "I'm aware of that. I've seen it before, with other students. And my brother had a crush on one of his teachers in high school. The point is, it was a crush, and he got over it. Six months from now Branko will be crazy about someone else."

"I'm afraid where you're concerned, we're not talking about a crush." His eyes swept over her face and figure, reminding her of the oddly intense way he'd studied her on Sunday.

Weakened by that look, she fought to retain her composure. "Why do you suppose Branko's attachment to me is any different than my brother's was for his teacher?''

"Because Branko wants you for his wife! In case you're in any doubt about that, take another look at the bracelet on your wrist!'' He stopped talking and stared at the rubies glinting in the light. She couldn't help wondering what intimate memories of the woman he loved were associated with the jewelry.

It prompted her to say, "Look, Mr. Antonovic. No one was more surprised about all this than I was.''

He studied her for an uncomfortably long moment, and she boldly held his gaze.

"Heather?'' The school custodian poked her head in the door, breaking the strange tension that stretched between Heather and Branko's father. "Just wanted to let you know I'm locking up.''

"I'm leaving now, Yvonne.''

"Okay. See you Thursday.''

He eyed Heather again. "My apologies for keeping you so long.'' In one quick, decisive movement, he gathered up her briefcase. "After you, Ms. Martin.''

Swallowing hard, Heather walked out of the room with him at her heels, turning off the lights as she went. Though they didn't touch, she was intensely aware of him and the faint tang of the soap he used as they passed the office and went out to the parking lot.

The last signs of daylight had faded from the sky. She could hear the crickets chirping and smell the sweet fragrance of honeysuckle. The warm summer night stirred her with inexplicable longings. For the first time she could remember, Heather had a presentiment of life passing her by, and she felt a sharp, fierce longing to capture the precious moments before they were gone.

Why she should feel this way tonight, she didn't know. But the visit to Zamura had unsettled her and made her think about the future. One that didn't include a child of her own. She tried to shake off her strange mood, concentrating instead on Branko's father and how upset he must be over his son's disappearance.

As soon as she unlocked the door of the Wagoneer, he opened it and placed the briefcase on the other seat before helping her in. Somehow, she mistrusted his faultless courtesy but wasn't quite sure why.

"Thank you, Mr. Antonovic."

He leaned against the door of the Wagoneer and placed his hands on the frame, repeating their positions of the previous Sunday. From the corner of her eye she could see the glint of his digital watch.

"Let's dispense with the formalities, shall we? Call me Nick." He reached into his back pocket for his wallet and pulled out what looked like a business card. Then he produced a pen and wrote something on the other side.

"If you're telling the truth and don't know where Branko is, I'd appreciate it if you'd get in touch with me the minute you do hear from him. Call me day or night. My business phone number's printed on the front. All you have to do is tell my secretary who you are and she'll put you through to me directly. I've also written down my home phone because it isn't listed in the directory."

"You may have a long wait!" she almost shouted at him as he handed her the card. Her fingers accidentally brushed his, bringing the nerve endings to sudden life. "You might have better luck calling the police."

His eyes became mere slits. "That's exactly what I want to avoid. I've been putting it off in the hope Branko will come home on his own."

"I agree there could be serious consequences if he got in with an unruly crowd. His naïveté could take him down the wrong path." She spoke mostly to herself, but he heard her.

"That's what keeps me awake nights. Of course it's possible he's joined up with a band of Gypsies in the area, and if that's the case I'm not as worried. My greatest fear is that he could end up at the mercy of some gang and ultimately find himself in trouble with the law. Unfortunately the Rom are probably the most misunderstood race of people in the world."

Heather knew he spoke the truth. Branko would have a hard time wherever he went, which prompted her to ask, "Has he had to deal with a lot of prejudice since coming here?"

"Some," he muttered. "But because I'm his father, people in this area tend to be more careful about what they say and do. Now that he's without my protection, he may decide life with me isn't so terrible, after all, and come back home."

Heather frowned at his statement, but instead of commenting on it, she asked, "Do you think he had any money with him when he left in the truck?"

One eyebrow lifted disdainfully. "You'd know more about that than I. It's possible he had a few dollars left over from his last paycheck. But he's not using it for gas money because, when no one was around, he left the truck at the mill where he works. He knew I'd be able to have it traced. Branko's an expert when it comes to eluding the authorities. His mother had a healthy fear of the police, and no doubt this was ingrained in him from an early age." He sighed deeply. "That's why I hesitate to ask for their help unless I'm given no other choice."

"I can't blame you for wanting to solve this on your own. I think I have some idea how Branko feels, because he even balks at filling out a simple form for the office. Mrs. Wood said he was paranoid."

"Branko's tribe was always on the lookout for trouble—they had to be. So paranoia is a natural response for him."

"That would explain why he hasn't formed many friendships yet."

"He has a good friend in his boss, Jack, who likes him despite Branko's rebellion against authority. And he's befriended a group of Gypsies who once camped on Priest Lake. But aside from them, you're the only other person he trusts."

"Not after Sunday," she whispered, shrugging helplessly. Without intending to, she looked directly into his eyes. For the first time she noticed the slight lift at their outer corners, a feature he must have inherited from his Slav ancestors. The shape of his eyes gave him a faintly cunning air, like that of a very sleek, very clever fox.

Suddenly she realized he was studying her mouth with just as much intensity. Embarrassed at being caught staring, she thrust her key in the ignition and started the van.

His dark brows slanted in a frown. "It's late. You shouldn't have to drive home alone through the forest at this time of night."

In view of the man's obvious dislike of her, his comment was totally unexpected. "I've been doing it for over six months now, Mr. Antonovic," she told him. She didn't add that Jay and her parents had expressed the same worry.

"Call me Nick," he asserted more firmly this time. "I don't care if you've been doing it for six years. What if something happened on the road and you were stranded? I think I ought to follow you until you're out of the woods."

His show of concern took her by surprise—but then she understood what he really meant. He thought she was going to meet Branko!

Flashing him an icy smile, she said, "Be my guest, but it really isn't necessary."

"I happen to think it is."

I'll just bet you do! she mused to herself. While he strode swiftly toward a silver Mercedes sedan she could see parked in the visitors' section, she glanced down at his business card. "Kaniksu Lumber Incorporated, Priest Lake, Idaho. Nick Antonovic, Owner."

She'd never heard of it because she lived in Washington, but the company had to be doing well if Branko's father was already this established after coming over from Yugoslavia.

The gleam of his headlights suddenly broke her concentration. Dropping the card into her purse, she backed out of her space and headed for the main street of Priest River. He stayed directly behind her and followed her all the way to Newport before moving up alongside the Wagoneer. Before he turned around, he gave a quick wave, but his unsmiling glance let her know he hadn't been convinced by her protestations of innocence.

Trembling with fury, Heather increased her speed. Yet when she saw his taillights flash in her rearview mirror as he finally sped off in the opposite direction, she experienced a peculiar feeling of aloneness, almost of loss. It made no sense at all.

She continued along the highway, a prisoner of her own tortured thoughts. Apparently Nick had been Branko's age when he'd fallen in love with a Gypsy girl, and Branko had been the result. Heather was troubled by the pictures that filled her mind and, to her dismay, realized she was attracted to Branko's father. She'd never met a man who stirred her, physically and emotionally, the way he did.

Why had a person of his sophistication chosen to leave Yugoslavia and settle in a remote section of northern Idaho, of all places? He was so different from Branko and probably appeared bigger than life to his son. Except for the slight accent, which Heather found attractive, she would have been hard put to identify his country of origin. Obviously he'd been doing business with the West for years to be this fluent in English.

Her mind churned with so many thoughts and questions about Nick and his son that she reached home without remembering much of the drive back to Spokane. She had the house to herself because her parents had gone to a movie, and she was grateful for the privacy. On the kitchen table she found a letter from her best friend, Heidi, in San Diego, but she'd read it later. Right now she wanted only to take a shower and go to bed.

As she undressed, she was more conscious than ever of the bracelet, the glimmer of its stones, its weight. "Oh, Branko," she whispered in despair. "Where are you? Why don't you come home?" With a sigh of frustration she headed for the bathroom.

Throwing her head back, she welcomed the shower's lukewarm spray on her face and hair. She clung hopefully to the possibility that Branko had befriended some Gypsies in the area, as his father had suggested. Just thinking about the Gypsies gave her an idea. The more she contemplated it, the more resolve she felt. The next day when she was through with her classes, she'd pay Zamura another visit.

The Gypsy had called her a *hanamika*. If she'd been sincere, perhaps she would be willing to provide some leads. Heather had no doubts the old woman knew a great deal about what went on in the Gypsy community. And at this point anything was worth a try because Branko had to be found as quickly as possible. The chance that he'd unwittingly joined a gang or some other undesirable group worried her more than a little. He might risk losing his immigrant status, and even Nick Antonovic, with all his money and influence, would have a difficult time extricating Branko from such a situation.

As she stepped from the shower, the telephone rang. Alert to the possibility, however slight, that it might be Branko trying to make contact, she wrapped a towel around herself, and ran back to her bedroom.

"Hello?" she said breathlessly when she'd picked up the receiver. As she did, she noticed the wet bracelet and attempted to pat it dry with the end of the towel.

"Is this Heather Martin?"

Her eyes closed involuntarily at the now familiar cadence of a deep male voice. It seemed to flow through her entire body in a jolting rush of pleasure. But immediately afterward came the ugly suspicion that he was calling to find out if Branko was with her.

CHAPTER FIVE

A TREMOR OF ANGER mingled with the inexplicable excitement that ran through her body. She pressed the towel against her chest to still the frantic beating of her heart. "Branko isn't here, if that's why you're calling."

"As a matter of fact, it isn't," he retorted, disarming her once again. There was a slight pause before he said, "I phoned primarily to make sure you'd arrived home safely, but also to let you know I had a talk with the head of the school tonight. In fact, he gave me your number. He told me that for the past six months you've been coming to Priest River at least half an hour before each session to tutor Branko, without compensation." There was another brief silence. "The two of you are even closer than I'd realized."

"I'm damned in your eyes, aren't I, Mr. Antonovic? No matter what I say or do."

"Not damned, Ms. Martin. I would be remiss if I didn't congratulate you on your accomplishments. Branko's English has improved markedly since he came under your influence. I plan to pay you for your services to my son."

"I wouldn't touch your money, Mr. Antonovic. Not one penny. What I did for Branko I did out of concern and a desire to help him. But of course I wouldn't expect you to believe that."

She expected him to counter with another nasty innuendo. Instead he said something quite different. "If you won't accept my money, then at least allow me to show my appreciation by taking you to dinner in Priest River before your class Thursday evening."

Gripping the receiver tightly, she said, "I'm afraid I can't. The class is having a party for Mr. Cheng. He's become a new father. I have to go in early to decorate and set up the cookies and punch before the others arrive."

"Perhaps I haven't made myself clear. Perhaps you've been telling me the truth. Perhaps you haven't heard from Branko. But after six months, you must have some idea how his mind works. If, as you say, your interest in him is purely professional, then you should have no objection to my bringing dinner to your room. That way we can discuss where he might have gone, where he might be."

His suggestion shouldn't have set her pulses racing. After all, she knew the sole reason for his persistence was his worry over Branko's disappearance. No matter how remote and unfeeling he had appeared in the beginning, Heather no longer doubted the strength of his love for Branko. Otherwise he would never have enlisted her help, despising her as he did.

"Class starts at seven. If you wish to come to my room sometime after six, we can talk while I get everything ready."

"Good. Now, one more thing."

A light film of perspiration broke out on her brow as she anticipated another cruel remark. "Yes?"

"Because I haven't put in an appearance at the school before now, you've assumed I haven't been interested in Branko's progress. But nothing could be further from the truth. Just for the record, when I registered him for night school, Branko made me promise I wouldn't interfere. He hates being treated like a child. From an early age, Gypsy mothers allow their sons a great deal of freedom. He's considered himself an adult practically since he was old enough to walk. I've had to honor my promise to him even when it went against every protective instinct I have."

Forgetting for a moment the animosity between them, she said, "Well, I can see how Branko wouldn't want you to accompany him to class holding his hand."

"You should know that better than anyone," he said smoothly. "Good night, Ms. Martin."

The fact that this was her parents' home was the only reason Heather stifled the urge to throw the receiver against the wall. Branko's father was the most infuriating man she'd ever met in her life. She'd never wanted to see him again after Sunday's fiasco, yet she'd just agreed to let him come to her class—where he would, no doubt, continue his brutal attack on her motives.

Making a concerted effort to put him and Branko out of her mind for a little while, she finished getting ready for bed, then turned on the television set. Unfortunately nothing held her interest. She turned it off again and climbed into bed, conscious of the heavy bracelet that had caused so much turmoil in her life.

With a sigh of defeat she slid beneath the covers, expecting to fall asleep as soon as her head touched the pillow. But troubling images of a make-believe world kept her awake until the early hours. A world in which a younger, carefree Nick played with his little son... and kissed his beautiful Gypsy lover...

Despite the next day's busy work schedule, Heather found herself watching the clock at regular intervals. At precisely three, she locked up her room, said good-bye to the school secretary and headed downtown in her Wagoneer.

She noticed an empty parking place a few doors down from the tearoom and pulled into it, unable to believe her luck. Usually she had to park behind her father's store.

She got out of the car and hurried toward the entrance. But her good mood vanished the minute she tried the door and found it locked. Too late she noticed the Closed sign propped in the window. Annoyed that she'd made the trip for nothing, she decided to go and see her father for a few minutes before driving home.

His downtown store was always crowded this time of day. Heather went inside and worked her way down the center aisle to the back where his offices were located.

Almost there, she halted in midstride. Out of the corner of her eye she saw the young Gypsy woman from the tearoom admiring a bolt of flame-colored satin. Without stopping to think, Heather walked over to her and greeted her in Romany.

The Gypsy looked taken back and said, "You!" in English. Immediately her black eyes flitted to the bracelet visible on Heather's wrist.

"You remember."

"Of course." She tossed her head. "Zamura said you'd be back."

Intrigued, Heather asked, "How would she know that?"

"Zamura knows many things."

"As a matter of fact, I just went by the tearoom, but it was locked."

"She's sick today."

"Tell her I'm sorry," Heather murmured sincerely. "I'd hoped to talk to her, because it's vitally important I find my Romany friend and I think she could help." The young Gypsy woman fingered the satin but wouldn't respond, reminding Heather of Branko when he was being obstinate. "He went off last week," Heather continued, "and his father hasn't been able to locate him since."

"Why are you telling me?"

"Because I must find him, but I don't know how to start or where to look. Are there any Gypsy camps near Priest Lake or Priest River? I'd be happy to pay you for the information."

The woman shook her head, backing away from Heather. "No. I cannot take your money. It is *bok*." Which meant bad luck. Her eyes returned to the satin material, and this gave Heather an idea.

"I can tell you love this color," Heather said, eyeing the crimson fabric. Branko had a sash fashioned from similar cloth. "Why don't we make an exchange? I'll give you what *you* want for the information *I* need."

"I cannot take anything from you."

"It won't be from me. I'll pay the clerk over there and she'll give it to you. That way it's from her, not me. I haven't touched it," Heather added on a burst of inspiration.

Clearly the Gypsy was in a quandary. She wanted the material. "You've never touched it?" she asked suspiciously.

"Never. I swear by my *vitsa*," Heather said, parroting Branko's words. It meant, "I swear by my family tree." He always used the expression when trying to convince her of something.

Heather could tell the young woman was considering her offer very carefully. "You pay the lady and she will give me the material. Then I will tell you what I know. But there are conditions."

Right now Heather didn't care about the conditions. "Martha?" she called to the assistant manager who was busy ringing up a sale at a nearby counter. "Would you help this woman as soon as you're through?" Turning to the Gypsy, she asked, "How much do you need?"

"Two yards."

"Give her three yards, Martha."

Martha nodded. Heather could tell her father's assistant was exploding with curiosity.

"I only need two."

"But if you had three, you could make something for your children."

The Gypsy didn't say anything, but Heather knew she was pleased. "If I give you information," the younger woman whispered, "you must not tell Zamura."

"Why?"

"Because she thinks you will make trouble."

"I wouldn't do that," she promised, attempting to reassure the young Gypsy. "All I want is to reunite a young man with his father."

"No police!"

"We don't want the police, either. Otherwise we would have gone to them in the first place."

Her dark brows arched. "Why do you care?"

"I'm the reason he ran away."

"Because his *dad* gave you the bracelet?"

"Because the young man gave it to me and I told him I couldn't keep it."

"Because you have the eye for his *dad?*"

The questions had taken a surprising new tack, one Heather didn't care to explore. Zamura had probably gossiped with her granddaughter after Heather had left the tearoom. Certainly the bracelet would have given rise to a great deal of speculation.

"I'm Branko's English teacher. He's been working hard to pass his test and eventually become a citizen. His father and I are afraid he'll get into trouble and be sent back to Yugoslavia. His father loves him very much and wants him to live here."

While they were talking, Martha measured and cut the material. Without Heather's prompting, she added two spools of matching thread and put everything in a sack, which she handed to the Gypsy.

"First you pay the lady," the Gypsy insisted, reminding Heather of her part of the bargain.

Nodding, Heather pulled her checkbook from her purse and wrote out a check for the exact amount. Martha stamped the back and put it in the till. "Now," Heather said, turning to the Gypsy, "will you help me?"

"There is a camp near Clark Fork."

"You mean on Lake Pend Oreille?" she asked excitedly.

"That is the one."

"Are there any others?"

"There is one more, but I don't know the name. It's on a river. You have to go on a lake first."

"Which lake? Think hard. Pend Oreille? Heyden? Priest? Coeur d'Alene?"

"I think it is the one with the French name."

"Pend Oreille is French. So is Coeur d'Alene."

"It has something do with with a heart."

"Coeur d'Alene!"

"Maybe." She shrugged indifferently. But Heather's thoughts were on the two rivers that flowed into the lake. She hadn't boated on either of them in many years.

"Do you know the name of the river?"

"I can't tell you any more. Now I have to go. Remember. You won't tell Zamura."

Heather eyed the Gypsy solemnly. "I promise this will be our secret. Thank you. You have no idea how important this is to me. The next time you come into the store, pick out anything you like and you may have it. From the clerk, of course.''

The Gypsy didn't smile, but her black eyes conveyed the first sign of warmth. ''First you find him.''

''Before you go, will you tell me your name?''

''It's Zara.''

''What a lovely name. I'm Heather, and I hope to see you again.'' The Gypsy gave Heather a slight nod before leaving the store in her spiked high heels and colorful outfit. Several people, including Martha, stared after the young beauty, who wore the distinctive Gypsy baubles and bangles with style.

''What was that all about, Heather?'' Martha asked when Zara had disappeared.

''It's a long story. I'll give you a detailed account one of these days. Thanks for handling things the way you did. I'll do something nice for you in return.''

''You do nice things all the time.'' Martha smiled.

With a feeling close to euphoria, Heather peeked in on her father, who was talking on the phone. Suspecting he'd be tied up for some time, she blew him a kiss and told him she'd see him later.

After running several errands in preparation for the class party the next evening, she drove over to Jay and Shelley's house on South Manito. Because he'd always been a boating enthusiast, Jay had a wonderful set of hydrographic maps of the Northwest, published by the U.S. Geographical Survey. Heather wanted to borrow them for a few days.

Shelley and Jay greeted her with open arms and invited her to stay for dinner. Heather accepted. While Shelley finished putting their meal on the table, Jay hunted for his maps, and Heather had the honor of putting Stacy to bed.

A little while later when they sat down to eat, Jay asked about Branko. Heather filled them in on the important facts, including her talk with the young Gypsy woman, but avoided answering Jay's personal questions about Nick Antonovic. The playful gleam in his eyes told her he wasn't satisfied, that he had every intention of foiling her evasion tactics.

After dinner they spread the maps on the table. Jay, who loved any excuse to pore over them, determined a number of possible campsites, highlighting the spots with a pen. The years of boating with her brother taught her to listen and take note of any advice he had to give.

When the grandfather clock chimed nine, Heather suddenly realized the lateness of the hour and said she had to go. After thanking Shelley for the delicious meal, she kissed them both and hurried out to the car. Jay followed her with the tube of maps, which he placed on the seat. As she'd half expected, he couldn't resist teasing her because of her unwillingness to talk about Branko's father.

Since Heather didn't have satisfactory answers to explain her physical or emotional response to Nick Antonovic, she preferred not to discuss him with anyone. Unfortunately she couldn't get his brooding good looks off her mind, not even during the next day's rigorous teaching schedule. She found herself anticipating that night's class with nervous excitement.

En route home she debated what to wear and finally decided on one of her favorite outfits—a silky print dress of blues and greens set against a white background. She knew it suited her figure and coloring, and felt a particular need to look her best that evening, a need she wasn't ready to examine.

Arriving at the house, she joined her mother, who was in the kitchen preparing dinner. They talked briefly while Heather made punch for the party. Then she excused herself to take a long, leisurely shower and wash her hair. With the aid of a dryer, she was ready by five, giving her hair a few last strokes until it gleamed a silvery gold and fell softly to her shoulders.

The rubies around her wrist glinted like hot fires as she rested her brush on the dressing table, and the bracelet instantly reminded her of the reason Branko's father was meeting her at the school. It was the jolt she needed to put the evening into perspective.

A more sober Heather gathered her briefcase and the things she'd collected for the party, then she left, telling her mother she probably wouldn't be home until eleven.

An hour later she pulled into the empty parking lot and hurried inside the school with some of her paraphernalia. As she made another trip outside to bring in the rest of her things, including the gift-wrapped sleeper she'd bought for the Cheng baby, the silver Mercedes drove into the lot. It parked beside the Wagoneer, and within moments Nick Antonovic emerged with a sack of food tucked in the crook of his arm.

The off-white crewneck and jeans he was wearing accentuated his build. She tried to ignore the sudden racing of her heart as their eyes held in silent greeting. Slowly his gaze traveled from the crown of her head to her long, shapely legs.

"Let me carry that," he murmured at last, relieving her of the bag of ice she was juggling along with her gift.

"Thank you." Quickly she turned away from his searching glance and reached inside the Wagoneer for the map tube, shocked to discover her hand was trembling. "I take it there's been no word from Branko," she said after shutting the door and locking it. He shook his head, mouth taut with strain. Together they entered the school and walked down the hall to her classroom.

He started emptying the sack, placing two delicious looking roast-beef sandwiches and a container of salad on one of the desks. "It's as if he's disappeared off the face of the earth," he said. "One of the Gypsies from around here occasionally works at the mill. He told me Branko used to go over to Clark Fork where a small band of Gypsies was camped. So I drove over there this morning, but saw no sign of them.

"A fisherman told me the park service ordered them to move on, and he has no idea where they went after they pulled out. It's like looking for a needle in the proverbial haystack. If Branko hasn't tried to get in touch with you by now, I have to wonder if he's even in the area anymore."

She could feel his pain and paused momentarily in her task of tying balloons to crepe-paper streamers. "I don't know what it would take to convince you I've been telling the truth," she said slowly. "Why would

I lie? I'm as anxious to find Branko as you are. I even consulted a Gypsy woman in town who told me where we might look.''

His dark head reared back. "How did you persuade her to *talk* to you, let alone tell you something like that? You're a *gadja!*''

"According to Zamura, I'm a *hanamika* because I'm wearing this bracelet. It's the main reason Zara gave me any information at all.'' She stood on a chair to begin attaching the finished streamers to the ceiling.

"What was the other?'' he asked.

She glanced down at him, smiling slightly. "A length of crimson satin from my father's store.''

"A skilled bargainer, hm? Maybe there's a streak of Romany in you, though one would never suspect it from a woman with hair the color of yours. Here, let me help.''

He'd been witnessing her struggle to tape the ends of the streamers to the ceiling tiles. In a matter of seconds he took over. But as he climbed onto a chair beside hers, his chest inadvertently brushed her shoulder, sending a little shiver of delight through her body.

She slipped down and methodically put out napkins and cups for the punch. It galled her to notice that he seemed totally unaffected by the brief contact while she was a mass of feelings and sensations, far too aware of everything she said and did. Only a fool would think he could ever have an interest in her while he still believed she'd been manipulating his son all this time.

She saw that he'd fastened everything in place and was returning to the front of the room.

"My brother, Jay, lent me his maps of the Coeur d'Alene area," she offered, nodding at the tube. "Why don't you take a look at them while I re-arrange the desk for the party? Maybe Branko's staying with Gypsies camped along the St. Joe or Coeur d'Alene Rivers. If my memory serves me correctly, there are lots of secluded spots."

She could feel his tension as he slipped the maps from their tube and spread one out on a desk, giving it his full concentration. After a few minutes he lifted his head. Even from the distance separating them, she saw his gray eyes darken with some emotion she couldn't name.

"I don't believe the Gypsy would lie to you, since she'd have nothing to gain and could conceivably fall into the Rom's bad graces if they knew she'd been giving away secrets," he told her quietly. "I have a hunch that if Branko is still in the area, this is where he would be. A river similar to those on the map ran through my grandfather's property near Skafja Loka, a mountainous part of Slovenia. He was a kind man who allowed the Gypsies to camp there whenever they needed a place to stay. Branko spent most of his life on the banks of that river," he murmured, sounding very far away.

"Is that how you met Branko's mother?"

"Yes." His voice was suddenly harsh—with grief, she supposed. "I spent all my holidays with my grandfather and was intrigued by the Gypsies, partic-ularly a beautiful young woman named Ibra. The summer I turned nineteen I stayed with my grandfather for six months and worked alongside him in his sawmill. But he knew I was enamored of Ibra and that several nights I didn't sleep in my own bed.''

Heather had wanted to know about Nick's life in Yugoslavia, but she cringed at the intimacy of the pictures his words conjured up. She didn't know whether to be relieved or disappointed when he changed the subject and suggested they eat before the students arrived.

He served her a sandwich and some potato salad, then prepared a plate for himself and sat down in one of the desk-chairs opposite her. He ate with a healthy appetite while Heather could only peck at her food, delicious though it was.

After a few minutes he raised his head and pinned her with a level gaze. ''I plan to search for Branko this weekend. I'm afraid you're going to have to come with me.''

Her fingers tightened on the fork she was holding. ''Why?''

''You've convinced me Branko hasn't made contact with you yet. But if you're truly concerned about his welfare, then you should have no objection to accompanying me. You admit you and your brother know these waters well, which would be an advantage. And if we do catch up with Branko, I'll need your help. He'll probably refuse to talk to me, but I can't imagine him turning you down, not while you're still wearing Ibra's bracelet. You'll be able to get through to him, convince him to return home, much better than I can.''

At his mention of the bracelet, the gold seemed to scorch her skin. "Mr. Antonovic—"

"Nick!"

"All right. Nick!" she almost shouted. "I want to find Branko every bit as much as you do, not only because I want him to remove the bracelet, but because I'm truly concerned for him. However, after the way he left your house, I doubt very much he'll be willing to talk to me, either."

What she couldn't admit was that her deep attraction to Nick made the thought of going anywhere alone with him intolerable. It was simply out of the question.

"Then we'll have to cross that bridge when we come to it," he said calmly. "This is your opportunity to prove me wrong about my assessment of the situation."

That did it! Sick to death of his suspicions, she pushed her food away, deciding to take up his challenge. "Fine. When do you want me to go?" she snapped.

A faint glimmer of satisfaction entered his eyes. "Saturday morning."

"Many parts of those rivers are shallow. I'll bring our family ski boat. It has a semi-flat hull and is easy to maneuver."

He frowned and something flickered across his face. "Perhaps I've been wrong in assuming Branko has had you out to the house before Sunday. Otherwise you'd know we keep a ski boat that'll be perfect for the search I have in mind."

"So that's where he learned to ski!"

Nick's dark brows lifted in question. "What do you mean?"

"Obviously Branko didn't tell you anything about the class waterskiing party I held at my house a few weeks ago. He was the star and he amazed everyone, including my family, with his skill. But none of us could get him to admit how he'd learned to ski so well."

He wiped the corner of his mouth with a napkin. "Branko and I have had some of our better moments together water-skiing, but he'd never give me credit for teaching him anything."

"On that particular occasion, I think it was more a case of showing off for the others than making a stand against you. Teenagers tend to think they know everything. He wasn't about to admit he hadn't come by his talent naturally."

"I'd like to believe that," Nick muttered. His expression altered, and he suddenly looked older, his face drawn and tense. "But the fact of the matter is he's made it clear, more than once, that he'd rather live anywhere than with me, as you saw on Sunday."

His comment brought to mind the ugly scene in his living room before Branko had stormed out. "Does Branko have a tendency to solve his problems by getting physical?"

He paused, his forkful of salad in midair. "I'm afraid so, but I must admit that he comes by it fairly."

"Why?"

"Branko was never accepted by the tribe because he's a *poshrat*—someone who's half-Gypsy."

"I haven't heard that word before."

"Probably because Branko's mother was possessive of him and told him to tell no one he's only half-Romany, which makes him an outcast. One of the Rom who'd always wanted to marry Ibra taunted her with Branko's illegitimacy and slapped him around. The more she turned the man down, the worse he treated her son. Branko had to fight for his place in life as soon as the tribe found out he'd been fathered by me, a *gadja*."

"How awful," she whispered, unable to comprehend the pain all three of them had suffered. "Couldn't you have done something to prevent that kind of abuse?"

Her question brought a look of incredulity to his face. "I don't know what Branko has told you, but I've lived on Priest Lake for the past eighteen years, completely unaware that I'd fathered a son. Not until last year, when Branko's mother knew she was dying, did she let Branko and my grandmother in on the secret."

"*What?*"

In a somber voice he said, "After her death, my grandfather took care of Branko as best he could, but his own health was failing and that's when he notified me. I arrived in Ljubljana in time to bury him and meet my seventeen-year-old son for the first time."

Heather felt the blood drain from her face, shaken by the revelation that Nick had lived all those years without any knowledge of his son's existence. It explained so much!

"I had no idea," she blurted. "No idea at all. Branko only said his mother and great-grandfather were dead, and that you were so full of grief you forced him to come to America to live. He said—" She broke off when she saw the grim look on his face.

"He said what?" Nick demanded in a deceptively quiet tone. "I might as well hear the rest."

She shook her head. "I . . . it isn't important."

"I happen to think it is."

Biting her lower lip, she said, "He told me he didn't like you because you were angry all the time about her death." Nick's eyes narrowed, giving him that cunning, dangerous look. She moistened her lips nervously.

"Nick, he never actually came out and told me you'd both come over from Yugoslavia together. I'm afraid I jumped to conclusions because I had so little information to go on. Mrs. Wood never said anything about your being established in the area all these years. I've had to make sense of bits and pieces of information Branko supplied."

He had moved closer to her, and she could feel the heat radiating from his body. "Then you might as well hear the rest," he said in a gravelly voice. "When Ibra found she had an incurable illness and was going to die, she was afraid no one would be there to protect Branko from the man who'd been mistreating him. In desperation she sought my grandfather's help."

"Thank heaven she had the foresight to do that!"

"I agree," he muttered. His eyes searched her face with a thoroughness that made her tremble.

"Excuse me, Ms. Martin? Where do I put cookies?"

Heather had been so involved in their conversation, she'd forgotten the class was about to start. The more she was learning about the Antonovics, the more she wanted to know, even if the mention of Ibra brought a pang to her heart.

Forcing a smile, she rose to her feet and greeted her student. "Come in, Mrs. Gutierrez. Put your things right over here." She indicated the library table, which had been covered with a festive cloth. "How are you tonight?"

"I am okay." The dark-haired woman smiled at Heather, then stared curiously at Nick. "A moment and I bring my gift." After leaving the cookies on the table, she disappeared out the door.

Heather turned to Branko's father, who by this time was on his feet and clearing up the remnants of their dinner. "You're welcome to stay and observe the class," she said impulsively, telling herself she'd issued the invitation out of professional courtesy only.

He shook his head. "If by chance Branko decided to show up tonight before class was over, my car would scare him off. And I doubt he'd relish dealing with both of us in front of an audience. In any case, I don't want to detract from the surprise you're planning for Mr. Cheng."

Heather didn't dare admit he had already done that. "Why don't you take the maps with you so you'll have time to study them before Saturday?" Without waiting for a response, she rolled them up and put them in the tube. She handed it to him, hoping he didn't notice how badly her hands shook.

His eyes played over her face and figure, sending a surge of warmth through her body. "I'll call you to make final arrangements. Be careful driving home tonight. A storm's predicted."

"It'll be welcome after this hot dry spell," she said, wishing her voice didn't sound so unsteady. "If Branko should come to class, I'll phone you immediately."

Frown lines darkened his features as he stared pointedly at the bracelet encircling her wrist. "I know that's not going to happen. To be truthful, I'm worried about something much more serious."

"What?"

His eyes lifted to her face. "I've been in Branko's shoes, so I know perfectly well how he's feeling right now." There was a momentary pause before he said, "I could understand, probably better than anyone, if he never recovers from your rejection."

CHAPTER SIX

HEATHER CLUNG to the nearest desk for support. *What was he saying?* That because Ibra still haunted his dreams, he feared Branko would suffer the same fate? How could he possibly equate his own love affair with Branko's teenage infatuation?

She could hear Nick say something to Mrs. Gutierrez on his way out the door, but Heather had no idea what it was. Her thoughts were filled with images of the Gypsy woman who had captured his young man's heart.

In light of this new knowledge about his feelings, any excitement at being with Nick Antonovic evaporated, and Heather was left feeling empty and depressed. But she didn't have time to dwell on Nick's past because, one by one, her students hurried into the room with their gifts and goodies. Everyone had come a few minutes early so they could surprise Mr. Cheng.

Branko's absence was noted, and she made up an excuse, saying he hadn't been feeling well; she didn't want anyone speculating about him or his whereabouts. Deep in thought, she almost missed Mr. Cheng's entrance. When he realized a party had been planned for him, the look of wonder on his happy face momentarily diverted Heather from her gloomy thoughts.

By the time eight-thirty came and he'd opened all his presents, she concluded that the party had been an unqualified success. Mr. Cheng thanked everyone profusely and promised to bring his family to class soon, so the others could see his new son. The room gradually emptied, with the other students helping him carry out his gifts. Shortly before nine, Heather had cleaned up the room, removing the decorations and straightening the desk, then locked the door.

She could smell rain in the air as she hurried out to her Wagoneer. Menacing black clouds reminded her of Nick's warning to be careful going home.

With vastly different emotions than when she'd driven to Priest River a few hours earlier, she made the trip back to Spokane in record time, beating the downpour.

Jay and Shelley were at the house when she arrived. The whole family was curious to know the outcome of her evening with Nick. But Heather was too upset to give them more than a brief sketch of Saturday's plan to search for Branko. After passing on Nick's thanks to Jay for lending the maps, she pleaded exhaustion and said good-night.

But Jay followed her down the hall to her room. "Hez, what's wrong? Are you sick?"

"No." She shook her head. "I guess the party tired me out more than I realized."

"I don't believe you." He studied her drawn face. "Something tells me this has to do with Branko's father. Want to talk about it?"

She started to brush her hair. "There's nothing to tell."

His teasing smile faded. "You can say that to anyone but me. Has he done something to hurt you?"

Heather put the brush on the dressing table and faced her brother, looking him squarely in the eye. "I suppose after the things I said about him in the beginning, I can't blame you for being suspicious." She took a quick breath. "The truth is, Nick isn't quite the monster I made him out to be. I'd say he's attempting to deal with a pretty insoluble problem."

"Branko's...unique, but I have to admit I liked him."

"Everyone likes him when they get to know him," she said, and found herself blurting out what she'd learned. "Given their history, I can't even begin to imagine how difficult it's been for Nick and Branko to find common ground. Now that I know more about Branko's upbringing, I'd say Nick showed remarkable self-control when Branko slapped him and he didn't retaliate."

"He's probably dealt with that kind of behavior on other occasions and is used to it. So, do you think Branko's going to come home?"

"I don't know, but I have to believe deep down that Branko cares about his father, if only because he knows his parents loved each other. Actually, after certain things Nick told me tonight, I-I'm convinced he never got over her."

Jay's shrewd gaze rested on her face for a silent moment. "How come they never married?"

Heather wanted an answer to that question, too. "I don't know," she whispered.

"Maybe that's at the root of Branko's anger, the fact that his father never married his mother and didn't live with the tribe. He could easily despise Nick for using her, or thinking her Gypsy background wasn't good enough for him. Maybe Branko wanted a full-time father and resented the fact he was nowhere around. If that's the case, it might explain the hostility toward his father now, and his unwillingness to cooperate. It might even account for the marriage bracelet."

"In what way?" she asked, her heart beating faster.

"Shock value. Maybe he deliberately didn't show up for work that day—because he knew his father would come home to find out why and catch you wearing the bracelet Nick had given Branko's mother. Maybe he gave it to you to hurt his father, to use as the ultimate weapon against him. You said yourself Branko went to devious lengths to lure you to the house."

Heather stared at Jay in amazement. "You've worked out a convincing scenario, but you weren't there to see the way Branko blushed when his father caught us red-handed."

"That's easily explained. As you pointed out to me, Branko's still a teenager and he genuinely cares for you, Hez. Guilt over using you in the battle with his father could have produced that kind of reaction. Nevertheless, he recovered enough to strike out at his father and insult him in your presence."

Everything Jay said made a strange kind of sense. "If you're right about all this, I don't see how Nick and Branko will ever resolve their problems. But no matter how angry Nick makes me because of his false assumptions, he cares about his son. I'd stake my life on it."

"That's quite a testimonial coming from you. Let him know that if he needs more help looking for Branko, Shelley and I are available."

"Thanks, Jay." She hugged him, then changed her clothes and went straight to bed. Despite the pounding of the rain against the windows, she fell into a deep sleep and wasn't aware of anything until the alarm went off at six-thirty the next morning.

She dashed into the shower and got ready for school in record time. Her parents urged her to eat breakfast with them, but she gave them each a hurried kiss and flew out of the house with her briefcase.

On the drive to school, she noted that the storm had passed over, leaving everything bright and fresh. She hoped today's good weather would continue throughout the weekend, since further storms would hamper the search for Branko.

The mere thought of spending a full day with Nick made her almost sick with excitement. What a bitter irony that the first man who'd ever managed to make her feel like this was unattainable.

Determined to put him out of her mind, at least until they saw each other again, she plunged into her work. At lunchtime she and a couple of other teachers went across the street for a hamburger. When she returned, the secretary in the office told her she'd had a call and handed her a slip of paper.

The second Heather saw Nick's name she felt a quivery sensation in the pit of her stomach. Apparently it was a long-distance number and she was supposed to call collect. Maybe he had found Branko!

Needing privacy, she arranged to use the phone in one of the counselors' offices and made the call. While she waited, she found herself contemplating the history of the bracelet that had once adorned the beautiful Ibra's wrist. Heather's thoughts flew back to the moment Nick first saw it on her arm and the way he'd—

"Nick Antonovic here." His deep vibrant voice suddenly came over the wires, jarring her from the painful memory. Heather could hear the operator asking him if he would accept a collect call.

Finally he said, "Heather? I'm glad I caught you before it was too late."

"Why? Have you had word about Branko?"

"No. I'm in Lewiston at the Idaho Timber Festival. This will be my only opportunity to make plans with you if we're to get an early start in the morning. Can you meet me at the dock in Coeur d'Alene at seven, or is that too early?"

"No. Seven will be fine."

"I had intended to pick you up at your home, but there's a meeting of the Associated Logging Contractors after the dinner tonight. I'm giving a speech, and since we'll be addressing some serious environmental issues facing the industry, the meeting will probably run late. I'm planning to spend the night here and I'll drive up to Coeur d'Alene at first light.''

"I'll pack a cooler so we don't have to stop for food."

"That won't be necessary. I asked you to come with me and I'll provide the groceries."

"Consider this my contribution for Branko's sake." She had to say it, if only to convince herself. Nick must never know how she was beginning to feel about him.

A long silence followed and she wondered if he was still on the line. "Nick?"

"Be sure to bring something warm. I've been listening to the weather forecast and there's a slight chance of rain before Sunday. Now I have to go. I'll see you at seven." The phone clicked before she could say goodbye.

Heather stared at the receiver in her hand, wondering what she had said to make him respond so brusquely. Maybe just mentioning Branko's name upset him. After all, if Nick was speaking at the convention, he had responsibilities he couldn't shrug off, which meant there was nothing he could do about locating his son until morning.

Troubled by the entire situation and the sudden fear that he was attending the dinner with another woman—maybe the one Branko had alluded to back at his house—Heather hung up the receiver. She felt out of sorts and wished she didn't have to return to class. This was one time when she knew she wouldn't be able to concentrate.

Two hours later, she left the school and stopped at a supermarket for groceries. On her way home she passed her favorite French bakery, and on impulse she stopped and bought some ham-filled croissants, which would make tasty snacks for their outing the next day.

When she arrived at the house, Heather delighted her mother with the announcement that she would fix dinner. She intended to make a pasta salad and fry enough chicken for their evening meal, as well as for tomorrow's picnic. While the meat was browning, she whipped up a batch of chocolate-mint brownies and a fruit salad, particular dessert favorites with the men in her family.

Around ten she went to bed, but to her dismay slept poorly and kept waking up thinking it was time to go. By five o'clock she decided to get up. She showered, then braided her hair into a single plait, which she pinned on top of her head. It was how she always wore her hair in skiing competitions. Her only concession to makeup was a touch of frosted coral lipstick, quickly applied after she'd eaten a bowl of cereal.

At quarter to six she was packed and on the highway to Coeur d'Alene, wearing a pair of jeans and a white T-shirt over her two-piece bathing suit. Years of experience had taught her to go out on a lake prepared for any eventuality.

The sky was lightly overcast, which could mean anything this early in the day. She pulled into the marina with its array of campers, vehicles and boat trailers, and discovered Nick waiting for her in the cab of a Ford pickup with the Kaniksu Lumber insignia on the door. Behind the truck was a twenty-one-foot olive-green-and-white Fiberform with a semi-flat hull, the perfect boat for exploring out-of-the-way places. At the moment, the fabric top was up, but it could easily be lowered if the sun came out.

Nick levered himself from the truck, and she saw that he was dressed in navy sweatpants and a matching T-shirt, clothing that did nothing to conceal his impressive build. His dark hair was still damp from the shower, curling at his neck and forehead. And there was a tiny spot on his chin where he must have nicked himself shaving. She noticed all this and more as he strolled toward the Wagoneer.

"You're early," he murmured in his deep voice when he reached the van's open window. His eyes reflected the gray of the clouds above. As he studied the pure oval of her face, emphasized by the upswept hairdo, he seemed to be searching for something, but she had no idea what.

"So are you," she said at last. Unable to sustain his intimate perusal, she glanced away, reaching for her purse to hide her reaction. The faint aroma of musk and shaving cream, combined with the natural scent of his skin, took her breath away.

Another second and she wouldn't be able to resist brushing her lips against the tender area on his jaw. From there it was only a quick movement to his mouth. An ache seared her body at the thought of that mouth closing over hers. "H-how long have you been waiting here?"

"Five minutes at the most." His disinclination to talk aggravated the tension between them.

Brushing the palm of one hand fitfully against her thigh she said, "If you'll get the cooler out of the back, I'll bring the other things and we can get started."

He didn't back away from the door. "If we haven't completed our search by dark, would you be opposed to camping overnight on the boat and continuing our search tomorrow? I've brought extra provisions and sleeping gear."

His question might have sounded casual to someone else, but in the undertones Heather heard the urgency of his request. He was desperate to find Branko and didn't want to waste precious time bringing her back to the marina if their one-day quest proved futile. To explore both rivers, as well as the camping areas along the shoreline of the lake, could take time, probably more than one day.

She'd certainly been camping with other men. But Branko's father wasn't anything like the fun-loving, easygoing boyfriends in Heather's past, men who enjoyed competing with her in sports and posed no threat to her peace of mind. Just thinking about Nick filled her with such longing it caused her heart to pound out of rhythm. She had a premonition that if she spent the night alone with him on an isolated river in the heart of the forest, her life would be irrevocably changed.

"Forget I said anything," he said, his voice emotionless. Without waiting for a response, he walked to the back of the Wagoneer to start unloading.

"Nick?" Heather climbed out of the car and hurried after him, anxious to reassure him that Branko was her first priority. "If I hesitated, it's because my sister-in-law's family is having a brunch tomorrow to celebrate their daughter Cindy's engagement. I'm supposed to help, but if I call now and make my apologies, they'll have time to get someone else." She had told the truth, at least as far as she dared without revealing the chaotic state of her emotions.

As he hefted the cooler, he sent her a piercing glance. "I wouldn't ask you to miss out on an important family occasion."

"Nick, they're Jay's in-laws, not mine. Besides—" her lips curved upward "—I happen to know one of the reasons they asked me to help is that the boy she's marrying has a brother home from medical school and they want us to meet." At those words Nick's grimace began to fade. "There's nothing I'd like better than to have a legitimate excuse to bow out gracefully. I prefer choosing my own escorts." What she didn't mention was that the marriage bracelet had become more than an encumbrance—it was an embarrassment. She didn't want to explain its presence on her wrist to her colleagues and students. And she couldn't keep wearing jackets and heavy sweaters at work!

Miraculously the first sign of a smile lighted his cloudy gray eyes. "In that case, there's a phone booth right over there."

She followed his gaze to the rest area several dozen yards away and nodded. "I'll call my mother and tell her I may not be home until tomorrow. She knows how important it is for us to find Branko, and she'll make the necessary excuses."

Before Heather had time to reconsider her decision or to change her mind, she called the house. Her mother responded with characteristic understanding and told her not to worry about anything but finding Nick's son. If she had reservations, she kept them to herself.

By the time Heather hung up the phone, Nick had loaded the boat and was backing the trailer down the ramp into the water. The confidence of his movements suggested long experience. Heather locked the Wagoneer, then slipped out of her jeans and ran down the ramp to catch up with him, conscious of his eyes on her long, shapely legs.

Quickly she tossed her purse and Levis into the boat and waded out in the water to guide it off the trailer. When she heaved herself on board, he shouted to her that the key was in the ignition. She waved to him before making her way to the front, then turned on the boat's motor.

Nick used sign language to indicate he would park the truck and meet her at the dock. They worked in perfect harmony, as if they'd done this many times before. Perhaps that was the most remarkable thing of all—with him, everything felt so natural. She'd only known him a week, yet in some ways it might have been a lifetime. Jay had said the same thing about Shelley after one date.

Disturbed by the trend of her thoughts, she drove the boat to the public pier at a wakeless speed, her eyes never straying from Nick as he emerged from the truck and strode quickly toward her. With every step that brought him closer, her heart knocked a little harder in her chest.

Before she realized it, he'd stepped into the boat and pushed them away from the pier. The next thing she knew, he'd moved to stand behind her as she steered them toward the buoys marking the inlet. She was painfully conscious of his nearness, of the warmth emanating from his body.

Hoping to distract him—and herself—she twisted around to ask where he'd put the maps. But the words died on her lips as she felt his gaze wander from her hips to the full curves of her body revealed beneath the thin damp T-shirt. Heat seemed to scorch her wherever his glance lighted, and when their eyes met, her legs threatened to give way.

She almost forgot where they were and forced herself to turn her head and focus on the expanse of water ahead of them. For the first time in her life, she was in danger of driving out of control. Another few seconds and they would have damaged the hull against a sandbar hidden below the surface.

While she concentrated on her driving, he settled himself on the opposite seat and folded his arms, establishing a physical intimacy she both craved and feared.

"Branko never stood a chance, did he?" The husky note in his voice made her mouth go dry, and she couldn't have spoken if her life depended upon it.

CHAPTER SEVEN

WHILE SHE FLOUNDERED, trying to regain her composure, he unzipped the windows to allow fresh air to circulate. "Tell me something," he said, breaking the uncomfortable silence. "What were you doing at the house the day I walked in on you and Branko?"

In an instant the tone of his voice had altered, becoming cool and remote. She shivered slightly in the morning breeze, not knowing whether to be relieved or upset by his change of mood. "I thought I'd been invited to a Romany celebration. He said something about a celebration for St. George and told me to come at three o'clock. Generally I try to attend cultural events involving my students because I want to understand them better."

Nick cursed under his breath. "St. George's Day is celebrated on the sixth of May. That rascal son of mine has absolutely no scruples when it comes to getting what he wants."

"You're right," she said, remembering Jay's warning. "There I was, eager to meet his parents whom I assumed had come over from Yugoslavia with him and probably didn't speak any English. I couldn't wait to try out my few words of Romany on them and brag about their brilliant son. And in case they had no money to speak of, I planned to ask the school for emergency funds so they could attend class with him."

"Instead, you were forced to tangle with me." Again their eyes met. His were intense and questioning. "Shut off the motor for a minute, Heather."

Though surprised by his request, she did as he asked, wondering why he wanted to stop. They were well past the buoys and on their way to the confluence of the lake with the Coeur d'Alene River, about half an hour away.

"Look at me," he ordered.

Nervously Heather turned in his direction, resting her arm against the steering wheel while she tucked one leg beneath her on the seat. "What is it?"

He was staring at her so strangely.

"Before we go any farther, there's something I have to know. You have to be totally honest with me, because the answer will ultimately affect all of us."

"All of us?" She shook her head. "I don't understand."

"You, me and Branko."

What was he getting at? "Would you believe me?" she asked, holding his gaze.

He raked a bronzed hand through his hair, his expression controlled and unrevealing. "If I thought you'd been lying to me, we wouldn't be together now." Heather could scarcely credit his admission. "Under normal circumstances I would never ask you this kind of question. But since we're dealing with Branko, it's absolutely vital that I be aware of the truth in case we catch up with him today. Depending on your answer, I'll know how to talk to him."

"What do you want to ask me?" By now she was afraid of his question.

His eyes bored into hers. "You've been seeing my son at least twice a week for the past six months. Is it possible you're in love with him, but have been afraid to admit it because of the disparity in your ages...and the fact that he's a Gypsy? Does Branko have any reason to believe you return his love? Is that why he felt confident enough to give you the marriage bracelet?" A tiny vein pulsed at the corner of his jaw.

Her answer was an immediate and emphatic "No!" It reverberated in the air between them like a live wire, igniting tiny fires in the depths of his eyes.

"But you do care about him."

"You know I do," she affirmed, her gaze darting to the bracelet. "He's charming and engaging, and this may sound crazy to you, but when he told me that both his *papo* and his mother had died recently, I felt the need to comfort him and dry his tears. I think I have something of a mother complex where he's concerned."

"*Mother* complex?" he whispered to himself, but she heard him. The expression on his face was one of incredulity.

Heather rubbed her temples. "I know it sounds odd, particularly since I'm not old enough to have a son his age." *Let alone conceive one!* To her shame, destructive feelings of self-pity welled up in her again. Taking a deep breath, she said, "The point is, I've never had any romantic inclinations toward Branko. Please don't compare me to Ibra and the love you two shared."

His face darkened. "The thought never entered my head. You're the two most *un*alike women I've ever known."

That pretty well said it all, Heather thought. She turned away, stung by his words. What did he mean? Was it as she suspected—he had loved Ibra so much he'd never been able to love another woman? Was Branko right? Did his father still mourn her passing despite all the years of their separation?

Nick's proximity was too much to handle. She had to say something, anything, to ease the growing tension. "I can tell Branko had a real fondness for your grandfather," she ventured. "He must have been a remarkable man to respond to Ibra's appeal and start caring for your son."

"As I mentioned before, he was good to the Gypsies and knew all about my infatuation with Ibra. Since he wasn't the kind of man to shirk responsibility, he did the best he could for Branko. My greatest regret is that he waited as long as he did to send for me."

"Why do you suppose he didn't let you know sooner?"

A deep sigh came out of him. "My grandfather knew I'd made a new life here in the States. And he wasn't at all sure Branko could be happy away from the tribe, even though he'd been treated as an outcast. But to my grandfather's surprise, Branko seemed happy to live with him, and they developed a mutual affection. His dying wish was that I get to know my son and love him. Naturally I wanted that, too, and so I brought him to Idaho to live. I hoped new surroundings would help him adjust to the loss of his mother."

Suddenly Heather didn't want to hear any more about Ibra. But some kind of compulsion prompted her to ask, "Why didn't you stay in Yugoslavia and marry her?"

He grimaced. "I'm a *gadja*, remember? The tribe had no use for me. To make things more complicated, she was older than I, probably your age now, and had been the wife of a powerful tribal elder who'd bought her with the bracelet you're wearing."

So that was where it came from! Heather felt inexplicably relieved by the news. Nick had nothing to do with the bracelet. Each day that she'd been forced to wear it, her curiosity about the part it had played in the saga of the Antonovics had grown. "What happened to her husband?"

"No one really knows. He died unexpectedly, leaving her a young widow, but a powerful one in political terms. However, she didn't grieve for him because she'd never loved him and hadn't even met him until the day they were married. But it would have broken every law of the Rom for me to take his place and become her husband."

"Why didn't she leave the tribe to marry you?" Heather couldn't help asking, fascinated by his story.

"The widow of a *baro manursh* doesn't leave the Rom to marry a *straine*, because that was what I was, a stranger, an intruder," he explained tersely. "A Rom marries another Rom to preserve unity and ensure the purity of the race. She would never have taken off the marriage bracelet for me."

The emotion in his voice told her that Nick Antonovic had lived through a tragic love affair at the most vulnerable time in his life. She could easily understand why he'd never found another woman to take his first love's place. The consequences of that love affair still affected him—in ways neither he nor the Gypsy woman could possibly have foreseen.

Inevitably her thoughts turned to Branko. Because Ibra had loved Nick, Branko had been abused by the man his mother continually spurned. What she had trouble understanding now was why Branko wasn't happy living with his own father, a man who obviously loved him.

Heather was so deep in thought she didn't see the approach of a large cabin cruiser. Before she knew what was happening, the wake rocked the boat, propelling her against Nick. For a fraction of a moment, she felt his strong arms close around her to prevent her from falling. She was instantly conscious of his hard muscled frame, aware of him in every charged cell of her body. And she wasn't prepared for her abrupt departure from his arms as he suddenly set her aside and began unsnapping the boat cover.

Reeling from the brief but intimate contact, she took advantage of his preoccupation to walk on unsteady legs to the relative privacy of the back of the boat. "I-I'll fix us something to eat," she stammered as he folded the cover and put it away, seemingly undisturbed by the incident. Without waiting for a response, she hunted for the box that contained the paper plates and other paraphernalia for their meal, willing her heartbeat to slow to its normal rate. Right now it was galloping.

While she prepared their meal, he took out one of the maps and sat down in the driver's seat to study it. A few minutes later she carried two plates of food to the front and deposited them on the dashboard, then went back for cans of juice.

As soon as she returned to the seat across from him, he started the motor and set the throttle at half speed so they could glide leisurely on top of the water.

Between mouthfuls of croissant and salad, which Nick appeared to relish, he used his binoculars to scan the shoreline for signs of people camping beneath the pines. At one point he spied a cluster of tents, but when they cruised by, the people turned out to be a local Boy Scout troop.

After visiting half a dozen campsites farther on with no results, they arrived at the spot where the Coeur d'Alene river empties into the lake. After cleaning up the remains of their meal and before heading upstream against the current, they consulted the maps and estimated they could travel for about twenty miles. Beyond that, the river was no longer navigable.

Nick was all business as they began to explore the meandering waterway. That one dizzying moment when she'd been held in his arms might never have happened and she was determined to put the incident out of her mind.

Occasionally they passed some fisherman casting from the shore, and once they met a group of kayakers. Each time Nick questioned them, and each time the answer was the same. No one had seen any Gypsies in the area.

They cruised mile after mile, scanning the semi-mountainous terrain with its lush wooded vales. At every bend in the river the boat could be pulled ashore, Nick got out to examine the underbrush for signs of a Gypsy encampment. Though most of the land was national forest, some of it was privately owned. When they came across homes or cabins, Heather and Nick knocked on doors and talked to the residents. But no one had seen any Gypsies in the vicinity.

By evening, they'd combed every inch of the river without turning up any leads. Branko was nowhere to be found. Heather could feel Nick's despair and tried to buoy up his spirits by reminding him there was still another river to explore.

At first he didn't answer and stared broodingly into the shadows cast by the firs. His mood seemed as dark as the clouds gathering above. Trying another tack, she suggested they eat while there was still enough light to see. At that, he expelled a heavy sigh and told her they'd better use any daylight left to find a place to spend the night.

Recalling a sheltered pond they'd passed a little earlier, he headed the boat downstream. They didn't reach the spot he had in mind any too soon. As they left the main channel and turned off into a small inlet surrounded by a dense windbreak of trees, raindrops as large as pennies were splashing down on them.

Nick cut the motor and let the momentum carry them to a grassy outcropping where they glided smoothly to a stop. Then he sprang from the boat, using the bow rope to pull their craft more firmly onto the shore.

While he secured the rope to the trunk of a tree, Heather pulled the canvas cover from the front locker and began snapping it in place. Moments later, Nick joined her to finish the job and light the Coleman lantern. Soon they were snug and dry inside, isolated from the rest of the world.

The rain beat a steady tattoo against the roof, but Heather couldn't hear it for the fierce pounding of her heart. The intimacy created by their confinement made her awareness of him that much more difficult to fight.

Thankful for any task that kept her busy, she stayed at the back of the boat, filling their plates with the rest of the food from the cooler. Every few minutes her gaze wandered to his handsome profile while he extended the front seats into beds and laid out the foam pads and sleeping bags.

He hadn't spoken since they'd left the main channel. The bleakness in his eyes revealed his somber frame of mind, and she had no desire to intrude. And, in truth, it shamed her that she could be entertaining thoughts of lying in his arms while Branko was still missing. She knew his son's disappearance was all that filled Nick's mind and heart.

Heather had never stopped worrying about Branko, either, but she couldn't ignore her feelings for his father—feelings out of proportion to the short amount of time they'd spent together.

"Dinner's ready when you want to eat," she reminded him gently. "Try not to be too discouraged. Tomorrow we may find him along the St. Joe."

Her remarks brought his head around sharply. "Do you really believe that?"

"I have to believe we'll uncover something." She attempted to placate him, recognizing that his anger was brought on by feelings of frustration and helplessness.

"Then you have more faith than I do."

Heather had no answer to that and carried their plates forward, placing his on the dashboard before she sat down to eat. The steady rainfall sounded louder than before, perhaps because she was reacting to the tension emanating from Nick.

She took a few bites of chicken, but found she had little appetite. If only she could get his mind off his son, even for a few minutes. "Nick, you haven't mentioned your parents. Tell me about them. I wanted to ask you the other night before my class, but there wasn't time."

He finished eating a drumstick before darting her a sharp glance. "Until I was nineteen, I lived with my family in Ljubljana. My parents were hotel keepers and insisted my sister and I learn English so we could help attract more foreign tourists. Secretly my parents hoped one day to emigrate to the West, but an earthquake in northern Yugoslavia demolished the hotel and killed my family before that could happen."

"How awful for you," she whispered. "Where were you when the quake struck?"

"At my grandfather's. But it was all a long time ago—almost twenty years—and the memory no longer causes me pain, so wipe that tragic look from your face. I stayed with him for a half a year, but at that point my entire focus was on getting out of Yugoslavia."

"You were young to be so daring!"

"At an early age, my parents' dream had become mine. I'd met some of your countrymen and they had painted pictures of the freedoms you enjoy. Their words made me restless and I told my grandfather I was going to America as soon as I could figure out a way to leave the country. I wanted him to go with me, but he said he was too old and wanted to be buried next to my grandmother."

"How did you finally get out?" Everything he said fascinated her.

He took the fruit punch she'd poured for him. "Ibra came up with a plan," he muttered before taking a long swallow.

At his mention of the Gypsy's name, the mint brownie Heather was eating turned to sawdust in her mouth and she put the rest of it back on her plate. Not only had Ibra captured his love, she'd been the one responsible for helping him attain his dream. *How could another woman possibly compete with a memory like that?*

Heather really didn't want to hear any more, but she was the one who'd brought up the subject, and ironically it now seemed that Nick was willing to talk.

"My grandfather's village was located near the Austrian border. The Gypsies often crossed back and forth undetected, or were able to bribe the guards with contraband. Ibra came up with the idea of hiding me in her *tsara*."

"Is that one of those Gypsy wagons?" Heather asked, caught up in the story despite her pain.

"That's right. Ibra's was very elaborate, another gift from her husband. No doubt Branko was born in it."

He paused to finish his drink. "Her offer appealed to me because she said we could head for the border immediately. With the impatience of youth, I leapt at the suggestion, unable to abide the thought of all the red tape involved in trying to leave the country through proper channels. Ibra's plan served me perfectly, and I had my grandfather's blessing, as well."

Heather stirred restlessly, wondering how Ibra could have let Nick go so easily. "Why didn't she tell you she was pregnant?"

His face became an inscrutable mask. "Every Gypsy woman wants to give birth to a son, and Ibra's marriage had been childless. With hindsight, I can see why she was so willing to help me escape. She knew she was carrying my child and realized she wouldn't have to share him if I left the country."

"But you were the father!" Heather cried out, aghast, envying the Gypsy woman her ability to conceive Nick's son.

His sober gaze searched hers. "You would have to understand her background. All her life she was treated like chattel, never possessing anything of her very own until her husband died. Those early years of poverty and deprivation turned Ibra into the kind of woman who would have killed anyone daring to touch anything that belonged to her. Where Branko's future was concerned, only the advent of death forced her to relinquish her fierce independence and turn to my grandfather for help. Even then, I'm sure it went against every drop of Romany blood flowing through her veins."

His words recalled something Jay had suggested, and prompted her to ask, "What do you think she told Branko when he asked about his father?"

She heard his sharp intake of breath. "I have no idea, but the tribe had seen me with Ibra and obviously didn't let her get away with saying Branko was her husband's child. Otherwise he would never have been so mistreated."

Heather's hand clutched the corner of the blanket. "Is it possible Branko thinks you deserted him all those years ago? My brother wondered if Branko purposely gave me the marriage bracelet to hurt you in the most painful way he could think of as...as a form of retaliation."

At the words, Nick put his half-empty plate on the dashboard and sat forward, clasping his hands between his legs.

"Your brother must have uncanny insights into people."

"He's a good attorney."

Nick nodded. "At this point I have no doubt that Ibra made up a story that painted me in the worst possible light. She had no use for men, and with good reason," he said quietly. "In retrospect, it's obvious that she used me to get herself pregnant, but I was too naïve and inexperienced to see through her plan."

"Even if that's true," Heather said on a shaky breath, "she turned to you in the end."

"And denied me the right to hear my son say *dad* for the first time, or watch him take his first steps." His eyes narrowed. "She knew I would never have left Yugoslavia if I'd found out we were going to have a child. But the one thing she had no control over was her own mortality. How she must have hated asking for help."

His distress let Heather see her own childless state in a different perspective. At least she hadn't given birth to a son only to be denied all rights to him throughout his formative years.

Unthinkingly she put a hand on his arm. "If that's true, then we won't stop looking until we've found Branko so you can explain the true circumstances of his birth. He's only eighteen. You both have the rest of your lives to draw closer as father and son. He cares for you, Nick, I know he does—otherwise he would have run off long before now."

Her action forced his attention to the bracelet encircling her wrist. She quickly moved her hand away again, embarrassed that he might guess how deeply her emotions were already involved.

"What will you do if we don't find Branko tomorrow?" she asked in a dull voice, not meeting his gaze.

"Call in the authorities. I should have sought their help the minute I realized Branko was really gone. It's been a week now and he could be anywhere."

She knew better than to suggest Branko might be at home waiting for him when he returned to Priest Lake. The truth was that Branko could be as far away as the West Coast, or Canada, or—

"You don't think he'd try to get back to Yugoslavia, do you?"

By this time, he was on his feet and starting to put things away in the cooler. "It's possible, but in spite of his Gypsy instincts, I'm afraid he wouldn't make it very far. Without money, it's tremendously difficult to survive here. Even harder than in Europe."

"How did *you* make it without money?"

"I'll tell you what. The rain has changed to a light drizzle. Why don't we go outside before turning in, and after that I'll try to satisfy your insatiable curiosity." To her relief, he didn't sound as brooding as he had earlier.

Twenty minutes later, when they'd changed into clean clothes and climbed into their sleeping bags, Nick turned out the lantern and began to talk. Somehow it seemed the most natural thing in the world to listen to his deep voice coming out of the darkness and know he was only a few feet away.

"As I mentioned once before, my parents managed a hotel, which was formerly a small palace owned by my family from about the mid-eighteenth century."

She shifted onto her side, facing him. "You mean you came from a monied background?"

"Somewhere way back, my father's family was titled."

"My mother's a professional genealogist. I'm sure she'd love to research a line like yours."

"Titles are common in that part of the world and mean less than nothing these days."

"Even so, I think it's fascinating that you're descended from aristocracy. Does Branko know about this?"

To her surprise he chuckled, and the warmth of it made her toes curl. "Titles mean literally nothing to my son. His mother taught him to be proud of his Gypsy blood, his *vitsa*. My family were *gadja,* and very poor *gadja* after they lost their wealth and power. Long before my parents' time, the government took over all personal property, and titled owners became part of the working class, which toiled for the welfare of the state."

"No wonder they wanted to leave!"

"Unfortunately getting out takes money. Lots of it. So my parents began catering to wealthy tourists who stayed at the hotel. Since the Yugoslavian *dinar* would be virtually worthless outside the country, they intentionally cultivated American and Austrian clientele and began to hoard currency from both countries. On school holidays, when my sister and I went to the mountains to visit our grandfather, Mother would sew the money into the linings of our clothes. Then he'd hide it away."

"Are you serious?" She'd read about such things but had never been personally acquainted with anyone who'd had firsthand experience.

He nodded. "This went on for years. My family lived frugally so every extra bit of money could be saved. Father was friends with a diplomat from Austria who said he'd sponsor us when the time came to leave. But the earthquake struck before that could happen." He cleared his throat and she sensed he was remembering the grief of that period.

"Because of Father's foresight and Ibra's wits," he continued, "I was able to cross the border undetected a few months later. I left in the dead of night and entered Austria with a good deal of money."

"Wasn't it hard to leave?" She'd been imagining his parting moments with Ibra, and to her dismay, her voice shook.

"No. Grandfather urged me to go and the taste of freedom was sweeter than anything you could imagine. I immediately made contact with my father's friend in Salzburg, and he introduced me to people at the American Embassy. The necessary papers were obtained and I was sent to Paris, where I boarded a plane with other refugees headed for New York."

"I can't believe all this has happened to you!"

"When I look back on it, I have trouble believing it myself."

"What did you do in New York?"

"We were put in government housing until our papers could be processed. It was the worst time for me because we had to spend so many idle hours waiting. I made friends with one of the officials. He spoke English with me and helped me get rid of my heavy accent."

"Your English is wonderful," she hastened to assure him, in awe of his flight to freedom and his many accomplishments.

"That's because my parents made my sister and me practice every day. My mother was a regular commandant," he added, but she heard the underlying love in his voice.

"How did you ever end up in Idaho?"

"Some people might call it chance. Ibra would have said it was destiny." The fact that her name still came so easily to his lips upset Heather more than she cared to admit, but Nick seemed unaware of her reaction.

"I did any job that brought work, waiting for the time when something would take me out of New York. I've never been a big-city person. Then one day an official told us there was a forest fire raging out of control in the northern part of Idaho. If any of us wanted to volunteer to help put it out, we could plan to locate there permanently. I grabbed at the chance to go."

"To fight a forest fire?"

"Hardly," he said. "I yearned for the mountains and forests of home. To me, Idaho sounded like paradise. You have to understand I spent a great deal of time with my grandfather who was an expert woodworker and ran the local sawmill. By the time I was sixteen, I knew how to do his job almost as well as he did. I figured I could find similar work in Idaho."

"You built your house, didn't you?"

"That's right."

"The shutters and the door knocker are beautiful."

"Those were part of my grandfather's house. After the funeral, Branko and I removed them when no one else was around and packed them up to bring with us, because they had so much meaning and would always remind us of our roots.''

And of Ibra?

Heather turned away from Nick, nursing a heartache too deep for tears, because she knew she'd fallen in love with him. It was as the old Gypsy woman had said. *A great man has come into your life... Together you will gain all the world has to offer.*

She lay there in silent agony because the first part of Zamura's prophecy had definitely come true. Nick Antonovic was a great man. The greatest, as far as Heather was concerned. But his past was still affecting the present, and even if Nick eventually found Branko and they became reconciled, Heather could see no hope of his ever coming to care for her. The Gypsy woman was wrong.

Wishing she was anywhere else in the world except so unbearably close to him, she willed sleep to come.

"Heather?" he prompted after a few minutes.

She decided not to answer him and concentrated instead on the sounds drifting from the forest. He would assume she'd fallen asleep. Right now she couldn't tolerate being reminded of a passion so great that Nick had defied the conventions of the Rom in order to have his heart's desire—Branko's mother. Perhaps it was easier for him to leave Yugoslavia than to stay, knowing he could never be Ibra's husband.

"I know you're not asleep. Something's wrong. What is it?" he demanded, sounding much more like the man who had come upon her and Branko that fateful day in his living room.

Grasping the first excuse that entered her head, she said, "You'd think that after teaching ESL for six years, I would be immune to refugee stories."

"Don't lie to me," he returned with an intensity that surprised her. "Are you nervous about staying in the forest overnight?"

"No...yes, maybe I am a little." She seized on his assumption like a lifeline. So much the better if he believed her. But a soft gasp escaped her throat when she sensed Nick's nearness and felt the air mattress give as he sat down next to her.

"Nothing can disturb the boat. Everything's snapped and zipped," he murmured, smoothing the hair away from her brow. She had undone her braid after he'd extinguished the light, but obviously that had been a mistake.

In the darkness she felt his touch ignite every inch of her body. If he didn't stop his light caress, she was afraid she might reach up and show him the true state of her emotions, embarrassing them both.

"Something else is bothering you," he persisted. His hand was gently stroking her neck and shoulder, covered by the thin T-shirt. "Don't you know you're perfectly safe with me?"

Oh—her breath caught—*she knew, all right.* The irony of his remark made her bite her tongue to prevent herself from blurting out the truth—that she was falling in love with him and knew he could never feel the same way about her. The pain sent a tremor through her body. Afraid he had felt it, she eased away from him and raised herself to a sitting position, but his hand was still in her hair.

"It's me, isn't it?" His fingers tightened in the silky strands. "You're afraid of what almost happened when you fell against me earlier. I wanted to kiss you." His voice went husky. "And so help me I still do."

CHAPTER EIGHT

"NICK..." His name had barely left her lips before she heard a groan. Then his mouth was closing over hers with a fierceness that robbed her of will. The sensation was nothing like her past boyfriends' affectionate advances at the door after a day filled with companionable activity.

The hunger of Nick's kiss sent shock waves through her body and she found herself kissing him back. She could no longer remember a time when she didn't want to taste his lips and be crushed against his chest.

He was so strong, so solid, she found herself clinging to him. Her actions put fuel to the fire consuming him, and suddenly one kiss didn't seem enough for either of them. While his mouth caressed every part of her flushed face, her lips fought for the same privilege. Each beat of his heart resonated through Heather's body, filling her with primitive desire.

Dazed by her feelings, she could only moan helplessly as his caresses became more urgent, awakening the sensual side of her nature. A smoldering ache transformed itself into a burning need only he could fulfill. She wanted to be the woman who could make him forget the pain and sorrow of the past. As if in answer, he took the hand caressing his chest and pressed a hot kiss to the palm. There was such intimacy in the gesture Heather's body quickened with desire and she searched for his mouth again.

Then suddenly everything changed as she felt the hand that had been savoring the soft underside of her arm slide to the bracelet and pause. For a heartstopping moment, Nick's fingers clasped it in a viselike grip before he tore his mouth from hers. There was the sound of ragged breathing, and then he rolled away.

In a jerking motion he unzipped the window on his side of the boat. The night air rushed in to cool her heated skin. She took several steadying breaths to regain her equilibrium... to come to terms with his rejection.

Obviously what had happened was nothing to him but the momentary desire a man feels for a woman when they're thrown together at close quarters. There was no emotional involvement. If she ever needed proof, she had only to remember the way he came to his senses as soon as he touched the cold metal of the marriage bracelet. Ibra had a hold on his heart that no woman could ever remove.

But Nick's lovemaking had changed Heather's life out of all recognition. If it hadn't been for the bracelet, she would have allowed the mindless abandon she experienced in his arms to continue. When he'd touched her, she had spun out of control, but never again would she let him get so close. From now on, she'd have to put on the greatest performance of her life to convince him she felt as indifferent as he did.

He finally broke the ominous silence. "Heather..."

"Nick, if you don't mind, I'm exhausted. Can whatever you have to say wait until morning?"

"Of course," he said fiercely. "I simply wanted to assure you that you have nothing more to fear from me."

"I was about to tell you the same thing. Good night."

After she heard him climb into his bunk, she fell asleep. To her surprise she didn't awaken until she heard bird song. When she opened her eyes, she discovered she was lying on her back staring up at a cloudless blue sky. The storm had passed over and a glorious sun was already warming the air.

Slightly dazed, Heather sat up and looked around, but Nick was nowhere to be seen. Not only had he lowered the boat's canvas top, his sleeping gear was stashed away and he'd transformed his bed back into the driver's seat.

Quickly she got up and put her own gear away before flipping the bed into a seat as Nick had done. Because she'd sponge-bathed the night before, all she had to do was wash her face, brush her teeth and braid her hair.

It was while she was pinning up the braid that she noticed Nick coming around the side of the boat. Dressed in a fresh pair of gray sweatpants and T-shirt, his hair windblown, he looked so wonderful she could hardly catch her breath. Still, she was instantly aware of his shadowed eyes and drawn face, which told her he'd probably spent a sleepless night.

"Good morning," she said a trifle nervously as he untied the rope and pushed them off from the outcropping. He muttered an unintelligible reply, then clambered over the front to take his place at the wheel.

"I've already had breakfast and want to get an early start. Do you mind eating while I drive?" His eyes glinted an impersonal gunmetal gray, withering her on the spot.

His icy politeness was almost intolerable after everything they had shared. "I'm as anxious as you to explore the St. Joe," she responded with equal coldness. "Let's not waste another second."

His jaw seemed to harden before he started the motor and backed up a little. Then he turned the boat around and headed toward the main channel. From there it was half an hour to the lake and another half hour until they reached its confluence with the St. Joe.

In all that time Nick said not one word. Heather might have been invisible for all the attention he paid her. When he finally did speak, it was to suggest she find herself something to eat while he poured more gas in the tanks.

Though she wasn't hungry, she didn't want to risk his displeasure, and so she got up to look for his cooler. With the lake like glass, she took advantage of the respite to make a couple of sandwiches from the cheese and cold cuts, and grab some cans of ginger ale. When they were under way once more, he thanked her for the food but didn't spare her as much as a sideways glance while they ate.

If his black mood was anything to go by, he'd obviously changed his mind about wanting her around. Still, she couldn't take all the blame. Branko's disappearance had worn his nerves dangerously thin. Today, if the fates were kind, he might come face-to-face with his son. Heather devoutly hoped so. She couldn't wait to be free of the bracelet, let alone Nick's proximity.

But with every bend in the river, her hopes sank lower because there was no sign of a Gypsy camp. In fact, except for a few people out pleasure-boating who claimed they hadn't seen any campers at all, it appeared their search had come to a fruitless end.

Had the young Gypsy woman lied to her? Heather had no answers. Desperate for any clue, she lifted the binoculars from the dashboard and scanned the forested terrain. But she saw nothing.

By noon they had gone upstream as far as they could and were forced to turn around and head back. Nick's complexion had a sickly gray cast that alarmed her, but she didn't dare ask him if he was ill. He stood at the wheel, his keen eyes sweeping the horizon relentlessly. Heather couldn't bear to see his anguished expression another minute and walked to the back of the boat.

She knelt on one of the seats and rested her elbows against the cushion so she could peer through the binoculars without getting tired. For ten minutes or so she rode that way, taking in every tree that moved in the wind, every bird that flew out of the bushes.

Suddenly she saw some horses partially hidden from view by a copse of pines, and a little farther up the hill, a fine thread of smoke curling from a camp fire. Her pulses started to race in anticipation. She had learned enough from Branko to know that many Gypsies kept horses.

"Nick!" she cried excitedly. "Stop the boat!" He cut the motor and reached her almost instantly. She handed him the binoculars. "Take a look over there."

He followed the direction of her outstretched arm and put the field glasses to his eyes for a full minute. "I don't know how we missed them before," he whispered. "Thank God for you." To her astonishment he clasped her around the shoulders and kissed her warmly on the forehead before hurrying to the front of the boat.

Within seconds he had the motor running again and they were headed for shore. Nick was out of the boat the moment she felt the soft scraping of the hull against the mud. While he tied the rope around a large rock, Heather slipped into her jeans and tennis shoes, still shaken from his unexpected display of affection, though she knew it meant nothing more than gratitude.

As soon as she'd jumped from the boat, he grabbed her hand and held on to it. She assumed it was a protective gesture so she didn't pull away. Secretly she craved the contact even though she'd promised herself to stay as far away from him as possible. He led her up the embankment into the trees. Closer now, Heather could smell smoke and hear the neighing of the horses announcing their arrival.

As far as she could tell, there were only two wagons. It wasn't as large a camp as Heather would have expected. When they reached the clearing, she counted two Gypsy families with their children, ten people in all. *Branko wasn't among them.* In one lightning glance, Nick's eyes communicated the same observation.

The colorfully dressed Gypsies made no gesture or sound of welcome. Except for the smallest children, all were smoking cigarettes, reminding Heather of Branko's constant use of tobacco. She smiled tentatively as Nick took the initiative and said a few words of greeting in Romany.

Immediately a ripple of reaction went through the group, and what appeared to be the oldest man slowly got up from a tree stump and came closer. His wizened face, framed by long grizzled hair, revealed a life of hardship, yet his dark eyes remained intelligent and watchful.

A dialogue began, with Nick asking one question after another, the old Gypsy shaking his head and grunting in response. The pressure of Nick's hand on hers tightened; Heather realized he was growing frustrated.

Her attention strayed to one of the teenagers. The girl, who leaned nonchalantly against a tree trunk, was pretty and slender like the young Gypsy mother at the tearoom, with a profusion of long black curly hair. But her gaze, fixed on Heather, was distinctly hostile. Heather frowned and the girl's hands went to her hips in a haughty show of disdain.

"I'm not getting anywhere," Nick said in a low voice. "I think they know something, but they won't reveal it to a *gadja*."

"Maybe they would to a *hanamika*," she said on a rush of inspiration, remembering Zamura's response to the marriage bracelet.

Nick's eyes sought hers for a brief moment while thoughts flowed between them, unspoken. Then the most amazing thing happened. When Nick said something in Romany and held her arm out in front for the entire camp to see, a voluble spate of Romany fell from everyone's lips.

The old Gypsy jumped back, as if he were afraid to touch the bracelet, reminding Heather of Zamura's reaction. Heather didn't need to understand Romany to know that Nick was pressing the advantage, using every argument imaginable to persuade them to reveal what they knew. He could be a magnificent, terrifying adversary, and never more so than now. Heather's heart pounded painfully with excitement just watching him, the *baro manursh* in action.

The young Gypsy girl wasn't quite so sure of herself now. In fact, Heather was positive she could read fear in the black eyes trained on Nick as the girl moved closer to her mother.

The old Gypsy scratched his beard and went over to discuss the situation with his wife, who wore the elaborate vest of the true *dukkerer,* or fortune-teller, with its stars and half-moons sewn on the hems and pockets. What would a Gypsy do without his hands? Heather wondered, entertained in spite of the seriousness of their situation. A sideways glance at Nick told her was thinking the same thing, if the almost imperceptible twitch at the corner of his mouth was anything to go by.

He squeezed her hand and winked. The gesture somehow alleviated a little of the despair that had been weighing on her. Finding the Gypsies had obviously renewed Nick's hopes. Taking a deep breath, she hoped the Gypsies would relent and tell him what he needed to know.

When she thought she couldn't stand the suspense another second, the old Gypsy came back to stand in front of them. He began a long tale, and with every word, every gesture, Nick's face tightened.

His hand squeezed hers painfully, until she wanted to cry out, sensing something dreadful had happened to Branko. Maybe the authorities had caught up with him.

When the old Gypsy had finished talking, Nick nodded his head in a sign of gratitude and turned to Heather, his gray eyes dark with misery. "Let's go," he ordered in a voice she scarcely recognized, pulling her along. Heather was so frightened, she could hardly breathe, but she didn't ask any questions. Nick would explain when he was ready.

Not until they had cast off from shore and were headed downstream well away from the camp did he cut the motor and turn to her. "I never did tell you how Ibra and Branko made their living, did I?" he began in a dull voice.

"No," she whispered, wishing she had the right to put her arms around him and absorb his pain.

"I didn't know anything about it until my grandfather told me. It seems that the Gypsies have their own caste system, and those who train bears are considered the lowest of the low."

"Bears?" One of the few animals Heather truly feared.

"That's right," he bit out. "Ibra's family came from a long line of *usari,* bear trainers. Apparently after her husband died and she'd sold all her jewelry, she no longer had anyone's protection and was forced to work at the only thing she knew."

"You mean like a circus act?"

"Exactly. But it's an act Gypsies from other tribes consider worse than begging," he murmured. "Her family lived outside Belgrade and picked up a few *dinar* entertaining crowds at various holiday festivities. As a young girl, Ibra would play the tambourine and the drum, and pass around the hat, the kind Branko wears, while her father forced the bear to dance on its hind legs."

"I don't understand," Heather said, trying to hide her impatience. His preoccupation with Ibra was distracting her. "What does any of this have to do with Branko? Have the Gypsies seen him?"

His mouth thinned into a tight line. "Apparently Branko made friends with this group a long time ago when they first camped near Priest Lake and has kept in touch with them ever since. It seems Branko has talked one of the men into helping him hunt for a bear so they can go into business together. Branko bought an old mare with the rest of his paycheck and the two of them left here on horseback two days ago to begin their search."

Tears filled her eyes to realize they had at least learned that Branko was safe. But to her astonishment Nick remained tight-lipped. "What's the matter?" she cried, shaking his arm gently. "I should think you'd be overjoyed to know he's safe and still in the area. You'll be able to catch up with him in no time."

"It's not that simple," he said, capturing her hand and holding it. "Because of what his mother taught him, Branko won't hunt for just any old bear. Of necessity it will have to be a black bear, and a young male cub at that."

Suddenly she could picture a she-bear chasing Branko and shuddered. "Does it have to be a cub?"

He nodded. "A bear must be trained from birth otherwise it will grow headstrong and never obey a human. At five months its teeth are filed down to the gums. While it's deathly ill from the pain, a metal ring is put around its neck.

"When the bear recovers, the so-called trainer inflicts more brutal torture by cutting or burning its paws so it rises up on its hind legs in pain. At the same time, he pulls on the metal ring with a chain. This way the bear learns to dance on its hind legs as soon as it feels the tug on the chain because it can't tolerate the pain."

"That's horrible!" She was appalled by the brutality he described, and it occurred to her that Nick's memories of Ibra had to be tainted by this ugly fact of her life!

"Training bears is dangerous and cruel. Now perhaps you have some idea how I feel about my son attempting to earn his living in such an inhumane way— apart from the fact that it's illegal here."

"But Branko can't be blamed for not having a conscience about it."

"Of course not. It's up to me to teach him better values and help him learn a worthy occupation. Unfortunately Ibra has seventeen years on me, and Branko may not live long enough for me to teach him anything. These mountains are full of bears, particularly grizzlies. If one of them cornered him, he wouldn't have a prayer.''

Feeling sick to her stomach, she asked, ''What are you going to do? How can I help?''

His hand abruptly released hers. ''As soon as I can deliver you safely back to the marina, I'm going after him.''

''Alone?''

''Well, I'm certainly not allowing you to come along.'' From his implacable tone, she knew he meant it.

''But, Nick—''

''But nothing!'' Effectively cutting her off, he maneuvered the boat as quickly as conditions would allow until they reached the lake. Then he opened the throttle and they flew at record speed past a number of ski boats and sailboats toward Coeur d'Alene.

The day was perfect, the temperature warm and growing warmer, but Heather couldn't appreciate her surroundings. Soon Nick would leave her at the dock to go after Branko. She probably wouldn't see him again for days, perhaps weeks. These few hours—yesterday and today—might be the only time she'd ever have alone with him.

Despite the sunshine, her body broke out in a cold sweat as she contemplated the dangers Nick would have to face if Branko found himself in trouble with a bear.

"Did the Gypsy tell you where Branko was headed?"

"No."

"Then how do you know where to look?"

"I don't."

"Nick—you're going to need someone to help you. There're literally hundreds of acres of forest to cover."

"I think I know how Branko's mind works. He'll track his bear in a densely wooded area filled with hidden caves, far removed from hikers and campers. That reduces the possibilities to a manageable size. Now, if you'll drive the boat alongside the dock, I'll go for the truck."

Heather had been concentrating so hard on what he was saying, that she hadn't realized they'd passed the buoys and were traveling at a wakeless speed toward the public pier. Nick moved out of the way so she could slip into the driver's seat. She noticed he was careful not to touch her, which only added to her misery.

It was midafternoon and the ramp was crowded with vehicles lowering their boats into the water. She understood Nick's urgency: the sooner he left Coeur d'Alene, the sooner he could start looking for his son. *Without her.*

As they waited for a boat to pull away so they could take its place, she thought she heard someone call her name. She glanced to her left.

"Hez! Over here!"

"Jay!" He and Shelley were standing on the pier waving their arms.

Nick's eyes flicked from Heather to her brother, and she heard him mutter something beneath his breath.

"What's wrong?"

His next comment startled her. "Obviously it wasn't all right that I kept you out on the lake overnight."

CHAPTER NINE

THE NEXT FEW MINUTES passed in a kind of blur as the boat slid into a vacant spot along the pier. Jay reached for Heather and swung her to the dock, giving her a brotherly hug.

"Our timing was perfect. Been having fun?" he whispered wickedly.

To her embarrassment, Heather felt her cheeks flush. She pushed Jay away and hugged her lovely, red-haired sister-in-law. "Where's Stacy?"

"We left her with my mom. I hope you don't mind us popping up like this, uninvited, but Jay thought we could give you a hand with the search. The whole family's worried about Branko."

"And with good reason." Her voice revealed her distress, provoking a puzzled look from Shelley, but this wasn't the moment for detailed explanations.

Heather turned around in time to see Nick alight from the boat. Just the sight of him sent her heart flying into her throat.

"Nick, I'd like you to meet my family," she said breathlessly. "Jay, Shelley, this is Nick Antonovic, Branko's father."

Everyone said hello. The two men exchanged steady looks, clearly taking each other's measure before shaking hands. "I assume you haven't caught up with your son yet." Jay always drove straight to the point.

"No. But thanks to Heather and your maps, we encountered some Gypsies who've put us on his trail. I'm indebted to both of you for your help." Nick spoke in a low, controlled voice, but Heather knew that Jay could discern the emotion behind his words.

"I'm glad to hear you've had some word of him, anyway," Jay said with genuine feeling.

"Except it's not good news," Heather blurted, eliciting a warning look from Nick, which she chose to ignore. "Branko's somewhere in the mountains hunting for a bear cub he can take back to camp and train. Nick needs to find him before he gets into serious trouble."

"Bear cub?" Jay repeated.

Without waiting for Nick's permission, Heather launched into an explanation, passing over the more unpleasant details, to give them an idea of what Nick had told her about Branko's past. "For obvious reasons he doesn't want the police called in. That's why he's going after Branko alone."

"You can't do that." Jay spoke to Nick in a no-nonsense tone, just as Heather had hoped he would. "I've hiked in these forests for years, but I've always made sure I had a rifle along in case of an emergency. Did Heather tell you I've offered my services?"

Nick stared at her for an uncomfortably long moment before focusing his attention on Jay. "I'm afraid Branko and I have imposed on your lives far too much already. He's my problem and I'll deal with him."

As far as Heather was concerned, his words were like a slap in the face. Now that she'd served her purpose, he saw no reason to carry on the relationship. That hurt deeply—but she still couldn't let him go after Branko by himself!

"As long as Heather wears that bracelet, I'd say the problem has become a family affair," Jay asserted, showing the same strength of will as Nick. "Besides, I've met Branko and I like him. I want to do what I can to help."

"We all do," Shelley chimed in. "He's a terrific young man."

Heather could have kissed them both on the spot.

"Look, I'm a new father, too," Jay confided with pride. His comment brought a reluctant smile to Nick's lips. "I know how anxious you are to have Branko back home again. So why not take us up on our offer? If you don't have other plans for the rest of the day, come home with us. We'll order pizza and put our heads together. I grew up in these mountains and I know them well. So between us, we ought to be able to figure out where that son of yours is."

Nick rubbed the back of his neck thoughtfully. "You're sure? What about your plans? I understand there was a family party today. I would hate to think you left it because I kept Heather out too long trying to find Branko."

"I'm not a child, Nick!" Heather regretted her outburst the second it left her lips. Humiliated because she'd revealed emotions lying too close to the surface, her eyes slid away from Nick's shrewd gaze.

Both Jay and Shelley flashed her a look of commiseration before Shelley said, "The party was over hours ago. And if it hadn't been such an important event, Jay and I would have invited ourselves along with you yesterday."

Nick rested his hands on his hips, studying Heather for a long moment before he turned first to Shelley, then Jay. "I appreciate your offer more than you know. But if I accept your help, I want it understood that Heather and Shelley have no part in the search."

"Agreed." Jay spoke so forcefully that Shelley gave Heather one of those "here we go again" looks. Jay bragged about doing his share of the housework, but he was protective of the women in his life to a fault. It seemed he and Nick were two of a kind, discussing them as if they weren't there.

Heather couldn't resist teasing. "Did you hear that, Shelley? Your lord and master has spoken. Thank goodness no man will ever be given the chance to put *me* under lock and key!"

Until she saw them staring at the marriage bracelet, she couldn't understand why Shelley and Jay suddenly burst into laughter. Then the absurdity of the remark hit her and she started to laugh, too. But one look at Nick and her amusement subsided. If the downward slash of his black eyebrows was any indication, he didn't seem to find what she'd said remotely funny.

"I'll get the truck and see you at the ramp in a few minutes," he told her coolly. Then he spoke to Jay and Shelley. "It might take us a while. If you two want to go on ahead, we'll meet you at your house. I'll follow Heather in."

Obviously pleased, Jay gave him a warm smile and clasped his shoulder. "I'll get out my topographical maps. We can plan our strategy while we eat."

Jay and his maps! She eyed him and his wife fondly as they headed for the parking lot with Nick. Heather knew she'd always be able to count on her brother. But yesterday, for the first time ever, she'd been thankful that he hadn't been anywhere around....

Last night's experience in Nick's arms was pure revelation to her. She had learned the meaning of rapture as their mouths and bodies became entwined. The sensation was so divine she'd been shocked when he rolled away from her.

It didn't seem possible he could stop doing something that gave her—and, she thought, him—such intense pleasure and not show the least sign of regret. If he had let her know he wanted to continue that ecstasy, she would have welcomed him into her arms and never, ever let him go.

But Nick's momentary aberration hadn't been repeated, and if he thought about their brief intimacy at all, it was obviously with self-reproach.

Aching with unassuaged longings, Heather mechanically helped him load the boat on the trailer and get it ready for travel. Afraid of her newly awakened feelings, she disciplined herself not to look at him any more than absolutely necessary and was thankful they were driving to Spokane in separate vehicles.

But once she was behind the wheel of her own car, the sense of loss became acute. They had spent al-

most twenty-four hours together, and she couldn't
fathom going back to a world that didn't include Nick
Antonovic. *How was she going to survive the rest of
her life without him?*

When Heather and Nick arrived at the house, Mrs.
Giles, Shelley's mother, was on the point of leaving.
Amidst introductions, Heather could hear Stacy crying in the background. While Jay walked his mother-
in-law to the car, Heather avoided Nick's probing gaze
by excusing herself to help Shelley. She found it ironic
that after spending so much time alone with him, she
should suddenly feel awkward and nervous in his
presence.

When she entered the baby's room, she learned that
Stacy was running a temperature and needed Shelley's attention. Relieved to have something to do,
Heather offered to make a salad and fix drinks to accompany the pizza, which would be arriving shortly.

She took the meal into Jay's study half an hour later
to find Nick and her brother poring over the maps,
discussing possible search areas. Totally preoccupied,
they thanked her, but kept right on making their plans
as they began to eat. Shelley, rocking her daughter,
was listening closely and even added an occasional
suggestion. Heather muttered something about not
being hungry and insisted on holding Stacy so Shelley
could grab a bite.

The five-month-old baby had come down with a
cold and, unless she was held, refused to be com-
forted. Grateful for the distraction, Heather cuddled
her niece and paced back and forth, enjoying the

warmth of her small, restless body while the others conversed.

Once, Nick lifted his head unexpectedly and stared at Heather. His eyes had gone a smoky gray color, and she immediately wondered if he was reflecting on all the years he'd missed when Branko had grown from an infant into a handsome young man.

"I can leave Tuesday morning at six," Jay said, drawing Nick's attention back to the conversation. "That'll give us tomorrow to get our gear together."

"Meet me at my office in Priest River, and we'll drive up in my truck from there. It has a power winch and anything else we might need."

Already anxious for their safety, Heather glanced uneasily at Nick. "Where exactly will you be going the first day?"

"Above Upper Priest Lake in the Kaniksu Forest."

"We know that area well, don't we, Hez?" Jay smiled at her as if he didn't have a worry in the world, but she wasn't fooled.

"Yes." *And it's full of grizzlies,* she wanted to say but didn't dare.

"Here. Let me take Stacy so you can eat." Nick changed the subject, reaching to take the baby from her arms. Heather had no choice but to give her up while a smiling Shelley looked on.

As naturally as if he had been the father, Nick cradled Stacy in his arms, and to everyone's amazement, she stopped crying and stared up at him totally absorbed. He grinned and put out a finger to stroke her silky, red-gold hair.

"I've been wanting to do this all night." His adoring smile made Heather want to cry. "Your baby's an angel. If you ever need a sitter, I'm your man."

"I hope you mean that, because I plan to take you up on your offer," Shelley said, clearly delighted at the prospect of Nick Antonovic caring for their daughter.

As Nick, still smiling gently, studied each perfect feature of Stacy's heart-shaped face, Heather felt a lump rise to her throat. Was he trying to imagine Branko at this age? Or was he thinking of Branko's mother with her black hair and Gypsy eyes...wishing they could have raised their son together?

Needing an excuse to leave the room, Heather gathered up the plates and glasses and carried them to the kitchen. While she loaded the dishwasher, she was conscious of a new pain searing her heart. Even if she, rather than Ibra, had been destined to become Nick's lover—his wife?—she could never have borne him a child.

"You forgot the salad bowl." Nick's deep voice startled her. When had he come into the kitchen? Right now his nearness was more than she could handle. Hoping her actions wouldn't betray her, she thanked him for his thoughtfulness and told him to put the bowl in the sink while she finished wiping off the counters.

"Since you're so busy, I'll say good-night here."

Her hand stilled. "You're leaving, then?" she managed to ask in a voice that came out sounding more like a squeak.

"I've imposed on your brother and sister-in-law long enough."

She stared out the kitchen window, afraid to look at him. "I'm glad Jay's going to help you find Branko. He's the best person I know in this kind of situation."

"He and Shelley are wonderful, but without you I would've been forced to call in the police last week. I'll never be able to repay you for all you've done." He paused. "If you can bear to wear the bracelet a while longer, I'm almost certain Branko himself will be able to remove it before very long and we can all get on with our lives."

It sounded very much as if Nick was saying goodbye. To her horror, tears sprang to her eyes and she clung to the edge of the sink, fighting for control. "I'm sure that day can't come soon enough for you, Nick."

After an uncomfortable silence, he said calmly, "You're right. It can't." In an instant he was gone.

The next few minutes took on a nightmarish quality as she heard him thank Shelley and Jay with what sounded like heartfelt sincerity before going out to his truck.

"Heather?"

She whirled around to find Shelley in the doorway, Stacy finally asleep against her shoulder.

"What on earth happened in here?" she wanted to know, taking in Heather's miserable face.

"Nothing," Heather whispered, but a sob in her throat betrayed her.

"You're in love with him. Jay suspected as much a few days ago."

Heather glanced away. "Jay's far too discerning for his own good."

"I think I'm a little in love with Nick myself. Heavens, any woman would be."

"Ah, but therein lies the problem." Heather's voice shook as she wiped her eyes with the back of her hand. "He's still in love with Branko's mother. No flesh-and-blood woman could compete with her memory."

"I think you're wrong. What's it been? Eighteen years? Love has to be nurtured, Heather, to be sustained."

"Then how do you account for the fact that there's no woman in his life now?"

"I can't. But then, I could ask you the same thing. How come no man has been able to get you to the altar before now? I happen to know several who've tried."

"Because I've never been in love with any of the men I dated."

"Exactly. Think about it."

"But after Ibra, any woman would fall short."

"How do you know?"

"Nick told me all about their love affair last night. She was older, and she was the first—and only—woman he ever loved. Not only that, she was his means of getting out of Yugoslavia."

"At seventeen most boys would be flattered by the attention of an older woman who found them attractive. A Gypsy would probably be quite irresistible. Exotic, forbidden fruit, that kind of thing. But if Nick had been truly in love, do you think he would have placed his desire to come to America above his feelings for her?''

"He didn't have a choice."

"Of course he did. Every man has a choice."

"But they couldn't marry. She had to stay with the tribe and he couldn't join it."

"But that didn't stop them from having an affair, did it?"

"No."

"Nick isn't the kind of man to be put off by impossible odds. I'm convinced he'd find his way around them—if he wanted something badly enough."

Heather stared at her sister-in-law, hoping more than anything in the world that Shelley was right. "What makes you so sure?"

"You can ask me that?" Shelley cried incredulously. "Have you forgotten I was only a week away from marrying Mark when I met Jay? The invitations for the wedding had gone out, the gifts had been arriving by the carload. It was my last nursing shift in the emergency room before the wedding and Jay was brought in with a concussion and that lacerated arm."

"I remember. It was awful." Heather shuddered. "I was driving the boat and suddenly this sailboarder came out of nowhere and crashed into Jay."

"Thank goodness he did," Shelley returned, her voice emotional. "Otherwise I would have married Mark and made the biggest mistake of my life! In fact, that's what Jay told me the next morning when I went to his hospital room after I got off my shift. I had no business checking up on him, but Jay made me promise I'd come and see him, and you know what happened from there.''

''I do.'' Heather smiled in spite of her heartache. ''When the folks and I came to the hospital two days later to take him home, he told us he had met the woman he was going to marry. Up until then, he'd been Spokane's most eligible bachelor and he somehow always managed to elude the state of matrimony. We couldn't believe it!''

Shelley nodded. ''The problem was, I desperately wanted to see Jay again, and he felt the same way. Only he had the courage to ask me to break off my engagement, no matter the consequences. And I agreed, because I knew it was the right thing to do. But Mark didn't understand and his family has never forgiven me—even though he's married to someone else now. I don't blame them, though.'' She sighed. ''Isn't that awful? After only one meeting?''

''No. It's not awful because you and Jay were meant for each other. And in the end, it was kinder to Mark, who's obviously managed to find someone else.''

Shelley nodded. ''I thought I loved Mark, but after meeting Jay, I realized the tremendous difference between loving a person and being in love. There's simply no comparison.''

''No,'' Heather agreed. ''When Branko introduced me to his father, I took one look at him and I haven't been the same since. The difference is that Nick has no interest in me beyond needing my help. In fact, when he said goodbye just now, he made it perfectly clear he can't wait to find Branko and . . . and get on with his life.''

"Naturally. How can he possibly hope to have a relationship with you while Branko's still missing and standing between the two of you?"

"What are you saying?" Heather's heart started to pound.

Shelley moved closer, a compassionate light shining from her eyes. "Put yourself in Nick's place. If you and your son were in love with the same woman, what would you do?"

"Nick's not in love with me, Shelley."

"You don't know that, and there's no way Nick is going to be able to do anything about it until he finds Branko and this whole situation is cleared up. Branko's tender feelings have to be considered before anyone else's, because Nick's that kind of man. Otherwise you wouldn't be in love with him."

"I knew it!" Jay declared unashamedly as he entered the kitchen. No telling how long he'd been standing on the other side listening. "So, it's finally happened to my little sister. Do you know what?" He gave her one of his crushing hugs. "I totally approve. Nick Antonovic is one in a million, and so are you."

"Jay—" Red-faced, she pushed him away from her. "You're jumping to conclusions. Both of you."

"Then look me in the eye and tell me nothing happened while the two of you were out there alone on that boat. Come on. Look at me," he persisted.

Memories of Nick's mouth devouring hers came flooding back with breathtaking clarity. She couldn't withstand Jay's courtroom stare and hurried out of the kitchen. His throaty chuckle followed her all the way to the study where she'd left her purse. Right now she needed to clear her head by taking a long drive in the cool night air.

Jay followed her to the Wagoneer and helped her inside, then closed the door. "One piece of advice, Hez. Don't be afraid to let him know how you feel. Men are extremely vulnerable and more terrified of rejection than you could possibly imagine."

Heat swamped her cheeks. "I don't see how he could be in any doubt about my feelings after... after..."

"So the ice lady has melted at last," he teased affectionately.

"Ice lady?" Her blond head reared back.

"Didn't you know that's been your nickname with the boating crowd over the years? Not that I've minded, of course." He chuckled. "It kept the wrong guys away, the ones I wouldn't like to see you involved with. And I knew it was only a matter of time until the right man came along. We're a lot alike, Hez. Destined to love only one person for the whole of our lives."

This man will be the only great love of your life, the Gypsy had said. Heather shivered.

"Jay, even if by some miracle Nick came to love me, it would never work out."

"Why?" He was perfectly serious now.

"You saw the look on his face while he was holding Stacy. He was cheated out of all those years with Branko... and I wouldn't be able to give him a child of his own." She couldn't seem to stop her voice from quavering.

After a slight pause Jay said, "There's such a thing as adoption."

"For heaven's sake, Jay. This conversation is absurd!" Pain glinted in the depths of her eyes. "There's not the least chance of my getting married to him or any other man, so let's not belabor the point. As far as I'm concerned, the only issue of importance here is finding Branko."

"Ignoring your feelings won't make them go away."

Her hands gripped the steering wheel till the knuckles gleamed white. "And giving in to them won't suddenly make Nick fall in love with me, either. Jay—" She eyed her brother anxiously "—please be careful. I couldn't take it if anything happened to you. I don't even want to think about how Shelley would feel."

He leaned inside and kissed the top of her head. "Nick's an experienced outdoorsman. Between the two of us, we'll find him."

"After class Tuesday night, I'll drive here from Priest River to find out if there's been any news."

Jay frowned. "We might be late getting back."

"I don't care. If necessary, Shelley and I'll wait up all night."

He nodded in resignation. "You need to go home and get some sleep. Don't worry, if Branko's anywhere in these mountains, we'll track him down."

"And put yourselves in danger!" Despite herself, the words came out on a wail.

Jay's expression sobered. "Your feelings for Nick run even deeper than I thought. I promise we'll come back safely—all three of us. Good night, Hez."

CHAPTER TEN

MONDAY TURNED OUT to be a torturous day, because Heather missed Nick with an ache that grew fiercer by the hour. Even though she knew it was futile, she kept going to her box between classes to see if there was a phone message for her.

She dashed home immediately after school and sat beside the phone, snatching up the receiver on the first ring in the hope she'd hear Nick's voice. By eleven-thirty she chided herself for being a complete fool and gave up the vigil.

Nick had no intention of making further contact. And why should he? What did he have to say to her, now that he had a lead on Branko's whereabouts?

Her parents urged her to go to bed. She knew they hated to see her get run-down from lack of sleep when she'd been doing so well since her operation. Heather had a long bath and crawled into bed, but she slept poorly and awakened before six the next morning, bleary-eyed.

A glance at the clock reminded her that Nick and Jay would have left by now. Unable to stay in bed any longer, she dressed for school, unable to swallow any breakfast. The hours passed so slowly she thought she'd have a nervous breakdown. She forced herself to eat some dinner, then drove out to the school in Priest

River. When nine o'clock finally arrived, she rushed out of the building and drove back to Spokane at top speed.

Jay and Shelley were still unloading Jay's Jeep when she pulled up in the driveway behind them. He stopped what he was doing and walked over to the Wagoneer, perceiving her question before she had a chance to say anything. "We didn't see any sign of Branko, but there's too much area to cover in one day. So, we're going out again Friday after work and we'll camp until Sunday night. With any luck, we'll find him then."

Her eyes closed involuntarily. "How's Nick?"

"If you want my opinion the man's in hell, but he doesn't let on."

From the look of him, Jay was exhausted. Though she had a dozen questions to ask, Heather didn't want to intrude on the little time he and Shelley had left of the evening, so she said she'd talk to him later in the week and went home to bed.

One day merged into another and the weekend came and went. Still no word of Branko. The second week passed much like the first, with Jay and Nick spending every available moment trudging through the mountainous terrain for evidence of Branko and his Gypsy friend.

When yet another weekend had to be devoted to the search, Heather's nerves were stretched to the limit. Not only did she fear for Branko's welfare, Nick hadn't attempted to see or talk to her, robbing her of what little appetite she had left after living through such a stressful two weeks.

By Sunday morning, she couldn't stand it any longer and talked Shelley into driving to the Upper Priest

Lake ranger station, where Jay and Nick had agreed to leave their truck. Not that Shelley really needed persuading.

Heather had to see Nick again and ascertain for herself that he was all right. Shelley admitted to feeling exactly the same way about Jay. Eager to be of help, Shelley's mother agreed to keep Stacy overnight so they wouldn't have to worry about getting back to Spokane at a specific time.

The ranger tower stood in a heavily wooded area reached by a twisting, turning dirt road no novice would attempt to negotiate. Fortunately Heather had joined Jay and his friends on many trips into the Priest Lake wilderness, and now she wound her way through the forest with a confidence that made Shelley marvel. Though it was a hot summer day, the air was much cooler beneath the pines. But Heather was too worried to appreciate the difference.

Almost at their destination, they heard the unmistakable sound of rotors, then exclaimed aloud when they saw a Rescue Flight helicopter from Spokane General Hospital soar above the firs farther up the mountain. It passed over their heads en route to the city.

"Someone's been hurt. Let's hurry!" Shelley urged in a trembling voice, echoing Heather's thoughts. It occurred to her she had never seen her sister-in-law so upset. Right now no one would guess Shelley was the best emergency-room nurse at Valley Hospital.

Growing more anxious every second, Heather changed gears and accelerated, not daring to speculate aloud on what might have happened. She was so intent on reaching their destination she almost drove into a truck barreling down the steep mountain road toward them. In an effort to avoid a collision, she veered sharply to the right while the driver of the truck stood on his brakes.

"It's Jay!" Shelley shrieked with joy, throwing open the door. Heather clung to the steering wheel, faint with delayed shock, not only from their near miss, but because she'd realized Nick wasn't with Jay. Sickness welled up in her throat as he hurried toward her with his arm wrapped tightly around Shelley.

"Hez, honey? Nick's all right. Stop looking so terrified."

"Thank God!" she whispered, then burst into tears. It took several minutes to get herself under control. Jay opened the door and hugged her. "D-did you ever find Branko?" she asked.

"Yes. A bear attacked him yesterday, but he managed to fend it off by climbing a tree. Branko said it would wander off and then come back. He didn't know if he could outrun it in his condition, so he stayed put, hoping his Gypsy friend would bring help."

"Poor Branko," Heather lamented.

"He's going to be okay. While I drove the bear away, Nick climbed the tree and brought him down in a fireman's lift. We made a stretcher and carried him to the tower, where the ranger called for a helicopter."

She lifted her head from his shoulder. "Is Branko badly hurt?"

"The bear clawed him in the leg and he lost some blood, but I don't think it's too serious. We'll have to wait and see. Nick flew to the hospital in the helicopter with him.''

She clutched his shoulders. "I've got to go to them."

"We'll all go. Do you think you can follow us, or shall we ride together? If you want, we can leave the Wagoneer here and I'll come back for it later."

"I'll manage fine," she said, wiping her eyes. "You go on with Shelley."

Jay smiled. "Stop worrying. The worst is over."

If only that were true, Heather groaned to herself as she turned the Wagoneer around and trailed Jay down the mountain. Depending on the extent of Branko's injuries, Nick might be even more distressed than before. And poor Branko! The thought of tangling with a bear terrified her. If she'd been in his situation, she probably would have died of fright, she thought, shuddering.

The helicopter was still resting on its pad when she drove into the hospital parking lot. She ran from the car to the emergency room, just behind Jay and Shelley. The admitting clerk told them Branko had been taken to surgery on the sixth floor and his father had gone up with him.

Together they rode the elevator, and Heather rubbed her hands nervously against her jeans. In a few moments she'd be seeing Nick for the first time in more than two weeks. Would he resent her presence? Would he consider it an intrusion? The blood pounded in her ears as she stepped off the elevator into the hall that led to the waiting room.

There were half a dozen people seated in chairs, but her eyes immediately found Nick. He was sitting forward on a padded bench with his hands clasped between his knees, his dark head bowed. Even in a soiled and bloodstained khaki shirt and jeans, he looked wonderful to her.

Putting aside her fear that he might not want to be disturbed, Heather walked over and sat down next to him. "Nick?" she said softly.

Slowly he lifted his head, as if he couldn't believe she was there. Without saying a word he stared into her brown eyes fringed with moist black lashes. The breeze had whipped her blond hair around her face and shoulders, but right now she had no thought for herself.

Two days' growth of beard seemed only to enhance his rugged features, yet his glazed eyes and anguished expression had aged him ten years. His eyelids looked heavy from lack of sleep, and new worry lines creased his tanned forehead. "How did you know to come here?"

She swallowed hard. "Shelley and I were on our way up to the ranger station when we met Jay. He told us what happened and we drove here as fast as we could." With her heart in her eyes she said, "I'm so thankful you found Branko and that he's alive."

"So am I," he murmured hoarsely, his gaze traveling deliberately over her face. Then his brows met in a deep frown. "Whatever possessed you to go up there when I specifically warned you to stay away?"

His question delivered in that stern tone infuriated her. "We couldn't stand by helpless any longer," she said passionately.

"I've known grown men who won't set foot inside grizzly country." His jaw went rigid. "Did Jay tell you that at the first sign of danger, the Gypsy accompanying Branko fled with the horses, leaving my son stranded? You, along with Branko, could have been the victim of a bear attack.'' His anger brought him to his feet.

His change in mood was so startling she didn't know what to say or do. Realizing it had been a mistake to come, after all, she got up from the chair and backed away from him. ''When Branko's conscious, please let him know we've all been praying for him.''

Nick had made it abundantly clear he wanted nothing more to do with her. Forgetting everything except her need to get away from him, she walked past a bewildered-looking Jay and Shelley with as much dignity as possible, then hurried down the hall toward the elevator. Unfortunately it was stopped on the second floor. In her present frame of mind she couldn't wait that long and opened the door leading to the stairwell.

''Heather, for the love of heaven, come back here!'' In the next instant Nick was racing down the steps after her. She heard the hollow sound of the door as it closed behind him. Though she couldn't possibly outrun him, she kept on going. The fear that he'd find out how destroyed she was by his repudiation made her run faster.

She had reached only the first landing when a hand closed over her wrist, bracelet and all. ''Where do you think you're going?'' he demanded fiercely, then crushed her to his chest. As before, when he'd kissed her on the boat, her body molded naturally to his. As before, her heart seemed to be an extension of his, beating with the same wild rhythm.

He cradled her head in his hands, and his eyes were like silvery flames scorching wherever they touched. "Don't you understand why I went a little crazy when you told me you'd gone into that part of the forest without protection? Oh, Heather..." he whispered.

Suddenly his chest heaved and she felt the tremor that shook his body before he lowered his head and found her trembling mouth with his own. The next thing she knew, he had backed her against the brick wall and for a little while she lost all control as they tried without success to appease their hunger for each other.

Heather forgot all about her promise never to let Nick get this close to her again. She forgot the impropriety of loving him while his son was still in the operating room, forgot to remember that his kisses didn't constitute any kind of commitment. The only thing that mattered was the feel of his mouth and hands and body....

After two hellish weeks of not seeing or hearing from him, her desire had reached a flash point. She couldn't restrain the way she felt about him, not with this intensity of need.

"Nick?" Jay called unexpectedly from the doorway. "Sorry to interrupt, but I knew you'd want to hear that Branko is going to be fine. He's been in recovery and now they're wheeling him to his room."

Heather had been completely transported by their kisses, and Jay's voice sounded muffled and far-off. Though the news thrilled her, she was still deep in the throes of desire and it took her a minute to respond. But Nick seemed to have no difficulty as he whispered, "Thank God," pulling away from Heather with a new light in his eyes. "We'll be right there, Jay."

"No." Heather avoided his penetrating gaze and shook her head. "You go ahead. You're his father and he'll want to see you."

A stillness came over his features. "You're wearing his mother's marriage bracelet. That guarantees he'll be expecting a visit from you."

"I can't see him right now." She felt panicky and edged farther away from him. Her lips were swollen, her cheeks flushed and probably showing a rash from his two-day-old beard. She knew her hair was a mess because of the wind and the way he'd been running his hands through it. Under no circumstances was she fit to appear in public, and certainly not in front of Branko.

When Nick didn't say anything, she blurted, "I...I need time to make myself presentable."

His grim expression said he didn't believe her. "Don't take too long," he warned, then kissed her astonished mouth with almost bruising force before taking the stairs two at a time and disappearing through the door.

His last kiss left her limp and trembling. She sank to the stairs and buried her face in her hands. Nick had kissed her just now as if she was his whole world. Maybe Shelley was right and he'd long since stopped mourning for Ibra.

But what if he didn't love her the way she loved him? How would life ever have the same meaning if she couldn't share it with him? What would be his reaction when he found out she couldn't have children? And there was Branko...

What made her think the young Gypsy could handle the news that she was in love with his father? Or worse, how would he deal with the idea of being her stepson after he'd offered for her in marriage—even if he'd had no real intention of following through?

The more Heather thought about it, the more she knew she had to get out of their lives and stay out.

Grabbing her purse, which had fallen to the floor, she jumped to her feet, anxious to leave the hospital before Jay or Shelley came looking for her. She dashed down the stairs to the next floor, then took the elevator to the lobby.

Under the circumstances, she had no qualms about leaving the hospital. Shelley and Jay would work out any transportation problems with Nick. Needing to be alone with her thoughts, she headed for the freeway, not caring which direction she took.

By the time she left Spokane, the afternoon traffic had dispersed and she had the road pretty much to herself. As the Wagoneer sped along the miles of freeway, she planned the rest of her summer.

School would be out in two weeks and then she'd go away until the end of August. It was time she accepted Heidi's standing invitation for a visit. Her friend was married to an architect and had been living in San Diego for the past couple of years. Heidi insisted the partner in her husband's firm was perfect for Heather. All they had to do was meet.

A week or two of lying on the beach and soaking up the California sun, surrounded by good friends, sounded like just the thing to put the experience with Nick into proper perspective. While she was there, she might even look into available teaching jobs. At this

THE MARRIAGE BRACELET 167

point, a change of scene would be welcome. And if she did decide to leave, she'd probably be able to get back at least part of the down payment she'd made on the new condo.

However, if worse came to worse and she had to teach in Spokane another year, she would be spared doing double duty, because a permanent ESL teacher had been hired at Priest River. He'd be starting in the fall. That would move her completely out of Nick's orbit.

There was also the matter of her condo, which would require time and effort to decorate. Much as she loved her parents, she missed having a place of her own. It went without saying that her parents deserved their privacy. Jay and Shelley were getting on with their lives. It was time she did the same thing.

To Heather's shock, by the time she'd mapped out a future that didn't include Nick Antonovic, she was approaching the turnoff for Moses Lake. She couldn't believe she'd been on the road close to three hours. After filling up with gas and grabbing a quick meal in town, she turned on a classical-music station and headed back to Spokane. A variety of Mozart concertos entertained her all the way in.

Moonlight gave the landscape a tranquil appearance and reflected off the river as she drew closer to home. Drained from the day's events and the long drive, Heather actually craved sleep. But she received a jolt when she turned in the driveway and discovered Nick's truck parked behind her mother's Volvo.

At the same moment, Nick himself emerged from the cab, looking bigger than life and, for want of a better word, dangerous. Maybe it was the stealthy way he moved that sent a shiver of apprehension through her body. What was he doing here? How long had he been waiting? Why wasn't he with Branko?

He'd apparently had time to leave the hospital and freshen up at home. He was clean-shaven and wore an impeccably white shirt and trousers, while she, on the other hand, had never looked or felt worse.

Heather had seen Nick in several different moods, but this was one time she couldn't gauge his feelings. His face gave nothing away. In fact, his very lack of expression made her wary.

He opened her door but placed his body so she couldn't possibly climb down without brushing against him, the last thing she wanted to do just then.

"Correct me if I'm wrong, but I thought you were going to join me and Branko in his hospital room this afternoon." His deceptively quiet tone frightened her far more than if he'd actually heaped verbal abuse on her.

Taking a deep breath, she said, "After you left me on the stairs, I started thinking about Branko and how important it was for the two of you to see each other without anyone else around. It didn't seem the right time for me to intrude."

His mouth drew taut. "He wanted to see you as soon as he knew you were in the hospital. Finding out that you helped search for him produced a smile that lit up his whole face. And when I told him Jay and Shelley were involved, too, he couldn't believe it. In fact, he's amazed so many people really care about him. After the loss of Ibra and my grandfather, he's been wary of giving his trust again."

"He's been through a lot of grief, but the most important thing is that he understands how much you love him. Have you made any headway at all?'' she asked anxiously.

He rubbed his forearm in an unconscious gesture. "When Jay and I scared off the bear and I climbed the tree to get Branko, he started to cry like a baby and called me 'Father.' In English, no less.'' His voice was gruff with emotion and Heather's eyes began to smart. "I'd say that went a long way toward a new understanding. As you said before, Branko and I will have the rest of our lives to grow closer and learn about each other."

"Oh, Nick, I'm so happy for you. When I think of him alone up there in the wilds, abandoned, at the mercy of a bear—"

"Shhh." He placed his fingers against her lips and caressed them. Only with the greatest effort of will did she refrain from kissing those fingers. "Thanks to you, we found him in time. He's safe and comfortable and will be going home with me the day after tomorrow. What happened in the past is over and done with. His recovery will be hastened if you'll make a point of dropping in to see him." After tracing the outline of her cheek, he let his hand drop.

Heather was on fire from his touch but didn't dare allow her emotions to surface. "I'll visit him the minute my classes are over tomorrow." When she saw his eyes narrow, she added in a softer voice, "I promise."

"For some reason, I'm not sure I believe that."

"How can you doubt it?" she retorted.

"I think I'm the wrong person to answer that question," he said, his voice strangely bleak.

She averted her face. "I'm sorry if my leaving the hospital without telling anybody created trouble with the car situation."

He shifted his feet. "It didn't. I drove Jay and Shelley home."

There was an uncomfortable moment of silence. "Are you on your way back to Priest River?" she asked.

"No. I went home earlier and packed a bag. I'll be staying in Branko's hospital room tonight. He's been taken off cigarettes, and I have a hunch he'll be climbing the walls at about three or four in the morning. Perhaps then I'll have the opportunity to tell him about his mother and me."

Heather only nodded. She was exploding with feelings and couldn't formulate words.

"Where did you go?" His question came out of the blue, but she couldn't pretend not to understand him. A palpable tension hovered between them.

"I took a drive. After the strain of the past few weeks, I . . . needed to relax."

"And did you?" he persisted.

"Did I what?"

"Relax?"

"Yes." *Until I saw you waiting in the driveway,* she wanted to shout.

"Jay told me you've been recovering from a serious illness. I had no idea, and I could shake you senseless for putting yourself at risk on account of Branko."

Anger made her cheeks flame. "Jay had no right to discuss my personal life with you!"

"He loves you," he said with enviable calm. "That gives him the right."

"Jay's never been one to beat around the bush, but in this instance he should get his facts straight, because I've been fully recovered for months. The doctor says it's only a matter of time before my energy level is completely back to normal!"

Too upset to stop now, she blurted, "Did he also tell you that as a result of my illness I'll never be able to have children?"

The silence lasted so long she began to think he hadn't heard her, though she didn't see how that was possible.

"Yes," came his quiet answer. "He told me that."

She could hardly breathe. At least now Nick knew the truth. She could feel his eyes on her face, but she refused to look at him. The last thing she wanted from Nick Antonovic was pity. "Jay takes his brotherly role too seriously."

"If I had a sister like you, I'd probably be much worse. You look exhausted. I won't keep you up any longer. For what it's worth, Branko and I will be indebted to you and your family for the rest of our lives. Sleep well, Heather."

AFTER INQUIRING about Branko at the third-floor nursing station, Heather walked down the hall to the end room and tapped on the door. She hated to disturb Branko if he was sleeping. To her complete surprise, he opened the door.

"Branko!" she cried, realizing at a glance that Nick wasn't with him. She didn't know whether to be relieved or devastated. "It's so good to see you again. I can't believe how wonderful you look!"

He was dressed in a green terry-cloth bathrobe that came to the knee and brushed the top of his walking cast. He was also wearing his hat, which she'd decided was the Gypsy version of a security blanket, and she was touched. Aside from his pallor, he seemed remarkably healthy for someone who'd had such a close brush with death.

There was something different about him, but it wasn't until he gave her a broad smile that she figured out what it was. The unhappiness in his eyes was gone. For the first time since she'd known him, he looked at peace, and that knowledge tugged at her emotions.

"Please come in and sit." He made one of his sweeping bows, removing his hat as he had done once before.

"Shouldn't you be lying on the bed resting?" She perched on the edge of a chair beside the bed. There were several plants on the dresser, including a brilliant pink azalea she'd had delivered.

"A moment," he said, maneuvering amazingly well on his crutches.

"I think you're trying to show off," she teased.

"I no am bad, eh?"

"You're terrific. Now, please sit down before you tire yourself out," she urged, and he finally complied, resting the crutches against the nightstand. "Where's your father?"

"Business. But he comes soon. You write name here?" He pointed to his cast and pulled a pen out of his pocket.

She grinned. "Shall I put Ms. Martin?"

"My father calls you Heather." He had trouble pronouncing her name. "You write that."

Astounded at the amount of communication that had already gone on between them, Heather wrote her name on the side of his cast. It seemed Jay and Shelley had beaten her to it. "Does it hurt, Branko?"

"No." He shook his head. "The bear no very big."

"The bear wasn't very big," she said automatically. He laughed out loud. It was a sound she'd never heard before. "You mad I am not at school?" There would always be an imp in Branko.

"I'm very mad. Mr. Cheng, Mr. Taheri, Mrs. Gutierrez, Mrs. Loumali—all your friends miss you very much and they keep asking where you are."

"Tell them I come—" he hesitated and scratched his head "—Thursday!"

"Good," she said enthusiastically. "Your examination will be in two weeks."

He made a face that left her chuckling before his black eyes darted to the azaleas. "You send flowers to Branko?"

"Yes."

"America funny place. Women send flowers to men. I like America."

She closed her eyes in an effort to fight the tears. "Have you told your father that? It will make him very happy."

Suddenly Branko's eyes narrowed and he regarded her shrewdly, as he had a habit of doing on occasion. "My father say you talk to Zara. Yes?"

"Yes. Your father and I spent many days looking for you. I finally asked the Gypsies for help. Do you know Zara?"

He nodded his dark head. "Zara is *hanamika.*"

"She certainly is, because she was the one who led us to you. I'm planning to see her and Zamura again soon to thank them."

Branko looked pleased, then deftly changed the subject. "You sleep on boat with my father?" His face was deadpan. Yet his question could have meant anything, and she grew nervous.

"Yes. It took us two days to search the rivers for you."

"You like my father." He certainly insisted on keeping to one train of thought.

"Yes," she said without hesitation. "Very much. And do you know why? Because he wants to be a good father to you and make up for all the years when he didn't know you were alive. He loves you more than anyone else in the world."

"He make bear run. My father no fear nothing." His pride in Nick told Heather what she wanted to know.

"That's right, Branko." She struggled to keep her voice steady. "He didn't care about his life. Only yours."

Through veiled eyes he murmured, "He has woman now. She very important."

Heather was thankful she was sitting down because the world reeled at his pronouncement. Did he mean what she hoped he meant? "Does that upset you, Branko?"

"No. She like Branko. We family very soon."

"That's good," was all she could manage to get out, because suddenly she couldn't be sure of anything. Maybe Branko was misleading her intentionally. She had no way of knowing.

Branko cocked his head and eyed her for a full minute before his gaze unexpectedly shifted to the bracelet. "You do not like my present?"

Sucking in her breath, Heather said, "It's beautiful, but I have a feeling your mother hoped you would give it to someone like the beautiful Gypsy girl I saw along the river."

To her surprise Branko broke out in another full-bodied smile. "You met Anika?"

"We didn't talk, but I saw her."

His chin lifted perceptibly. "She like Branko."

Heather thought as much. She couldn't imagine many young men more attractive than Branko. "And what about you? Do you like her?"

"She not too bad."

"Maybe one day she'll wish to wear a bracelet like your mother's."

Branko shrugged and leaned forward. "Please give me your hand." Almost afraid to breathe she extended her arm. In the space of a heartbeat, Branko lifted one of the mesh filaments at a right angle, and like magic the bracelet came apart in his hands. He winked conspiratorially.

"Thank you," she whispered in relief.

He nodded. "You do something for Branko?"

"Of course."

"I go home tomorrow. You come to Priest Lake. See Branko. Yes?"

She bit her lip. Much as she cared for Branko, she wanted Nick to be the one who invited her to their home. "Tomorrow's Monday. I won't be in Priest River until Tuesday."

"Then you come Tuesday. I study for ex-am-ination. Two weeks." He held up two fingers. "You teach Branko. Please?"

Branko had a way of getting to her, and in his weakened condition she was disposed to grant him almost anything. "Tuesday is too soon for you to have visitors. I'll try to make it on Thursday. If I do come, it'll have to be after my last class in Spokane, around four-thirty." Perhaps Nick would get in touch with her before then and she could tell him about Branko's invitation.

"Good. I search..." He paused and smiled so sweetly at her, she saw Nick written all over him. "I *look* for you."

"Oh, Branko!" On a rush of feeling she hugged him around the shoulders, then ran straight from the room into Jay's arms. Trust her brother to take time out from his busy day to check on Branko. He truly was a wonderful person. She couldn't stay mad at him for talking frankly to Nick.

"Hez!" He smiled down at her. "Where did you disappear to yesterday? Nick was half out of his mind when you didn't show up."

Not willing to reveal anything until she saw Nick again, she said, "I didn't want to intrude on father and son. They needed time together. That's why I came today. Branko and I had a good visit and he took back the bracelet.''

Jay's gaze flicked to her bare wrist before giving her a speculative stare. ''That must be a huge relief. But why do I get the feeling something's wrong?''

''What could be wrong?'' She favored him with her brightest smile. ''I've never seen Branko so happy. He and Nick have reconciled.''

''That *is* good news,'' Jay murmured sincerely.

''The best. But now I've got to go. See you later.'' She gave her bewildered-looking brother a peck on the cheek and hurried down the hall, unwilling to prolong their conversation until she had answers only Nick could give.

The next few days passed without so much as a phone call from him. Thursday, Heather still hadn't heard from Nick. She was in so much pain she didn't know what to think. It seemed Branko had been making a joke at her expense. She doubted she would ever fully understand how his mind worked and wished she hadn't agreed to visit him that evening, for fear of running into Nick.

But her fears appeared to be groundless, because no cars were in the driveway when she pulled up in front of his house. She should have been relieved Nick was still at work. Yet all she could feel was bitter disappointment, because deep inside she'd been aching to see him again, hoping desperately that he felt the same way.

When the front door opened, she stood there, staring helplessly at the handsome man standing before her, dressed in a pair of ancient cutoffs and nothing else. She found herself taking in Nick's hard-muscled physique and the rugged lines of his face.

Judging by the dumbfounded expression on his face, she was the last person he had expected to see on his doorstep, and this caused her heart to plummet. "I'm sorry to disturb you." Nervously she slipped her hands into the pockets of her cinnamon-brown sundress. "I didn't think you were home."

Apparently her explanation didn't please him. "The company can run without my help for a few days. Right now Branko needs me."

"I couldn't agree with you more. He must have forgotten he asked me to drop by this afternoon and tutor him for his final exam."

His eyes darkened to slate as they watched the play of sunlight on her ash-blond hair. "I'm afraid that will be impossible. After lunch he complained of pain so I made him take the medicine the doctor sent home with us. When I went to the *tsara* to check on him just now, he was in a deep sleep."

"*Tsara?*"

"It's a bow-topped Gypsy wagon."

Her eyes widened in astonishment. "How did he come by one of those?"

"About six months ago I asked a friend in Yugoslavia to look around for a used *tsara* and ship it to me, without Branko's knowledge, of course. I've been restoring it in my spare time."

"Where?"

"In one of the lumberyard warehouses."

"But that's fantastic! His own private hidey-hole. Jay felt the same way about the tent Daddy gave him years ago. I think there's a little Gypsy in every man.

Does Branko love it? I can just picture him lying on purple satin, wearing his fedora, king of the Gypsies.'' She knew she was talking too fast, but she couldn't seem to stop herself.

Nick's mouth turned up at one corner. "He hasn't been inside the house since I first showed it to him. I believe my welcome-home present was a bigger success than a boy's first electric-train set."

"Oh, Nick, you couldn't have thought of anything more wonderful. I wish I could have seen his face."

Inexplicably Nick's expression sobered. "I believe you really love Branko."

Surely he wasn't still suspicious of her feelings after everything they had been through. His comment didn't deserve an explanation. "I do," was all she said, swallowing with difficulty. "When he wakes up, will you please give him this little welcome-home present from me?"

She pulled a piece of jewelry from her pocket. "Tell him this pin is to be worn on his hat. It's a white columbine made from porcelain and gold, the kind of flower that grows in Idaho. He's a child of nature. I hope it will appeal to him and bring him *bok*."

She started to hand it to Nick, but didn't understand when he suddenly grabbed her wrist. In her shock, she dropped the pin to the floor.

"The bracelet! It's gone!" He tightened his hold.

Her gaze flew to his. The strange look in those smoky eyes made her tremble. "Yes. Branko took it back on Sunday."

"Sunday?"

"Yes. The day I went to visit him in the hospital. He's crazy about a Gypsy girl named Anika. I wouldn't be surprised if you saw it adorning her wrist one of these days.''

"Anika?"

Heather could hardly think when her hand was shackled to his like this. "Hasn't Branko told you about her yet? The pretty one at the Gypsy camp along the St. Joe?" She noticed Nick's breathing sounded as shallow as hers.

"He made a nebulous remark about deciding to keep his job at the mill because he needed money to get married when he became a citizen. I assumed..."

"It sounds like Branko has done some hard thinking and is planning for his future," she said. "After all, he doesn't want to be a burden to you."

"A burden?" He frowned.

"H-he realizes you have your own life to lead."

"What are you saying?" In the next breath his hands went to her shoulders, caressing the bare skin beneath the straps of her sundress. Heather thought she would faint from the sensation. She tried to pull away from him, but his strong hands held her in place.

"Branko said you had a woman who was important to you and soon you would be a fam..." The words died on her lips and she let her eyes ask the question she was afraid to voice aloud. In that brief tension-filled moment, Branko made a noisy, unexpected appearance behind his father. Nick's head swiveled around sharply.

Branko grinned at both of them, leaning on his crutches with a mischievous look in his black eyes. The marriage bracelet dangled from his fingers.

"Take it, Father. Give to Heather. She your woman now. Branko give *this* to Anika." Using one of the crutches for support, he leaned over and picked up the pin, feeling the satiny smoothness with his fingers.

"Branko Antonovic!" Heather cried indignantly. He'd been playing games with both of them. "You're shameless! Do you know that?" She was really furious with the young Gypsy. He still had a long way to go before he'd be grown up.

Her dark gaze swung to Nick's. She expected him to chastise his meddling, eavesdropping son. But to her complete surprise, laughter started to rumble out of him, a deep, happy laughter that rang through the forest and sent a couple of chipmunks scrambling up the trunk of a nearby tree.

In the next instant the world tilted crazily as Nick picked her up in his arms. "I appreciate the offer, son," he murmured, his eyes devouring her, "but I'd rather have the use of your *tsara*. Heather and I need a place to be alone and undisturbed for a little while."

"Nick! Please! Put me down," she begged, her face a brilliant shade of red.

Branko was enjoying her discomfort immensely. "I stay in house." He gave his father a conspiratorial wink, ignoring Heather. "I swear it by my *vitsa*."

With so many feelings and questions converging at once, she was scarcely aware of being carried down the stairs and around the back of the house. She wrapped her arms around his bronzed neck, breathing in the natural scent of his body and the tangy soap clinging to his skin.

When they were a few hundred yards from the house, she caught sight of a gleaming black-and-gold Gypsy wagon partially hidden by a stand of Noble firs. "Nick, it's magnificent!" She gasped in awe as they drew closer. Bouquets of colorful wildflowers were painted in exquisite detail on the various panels. And above the curtained windows was a plaque with gold lettering: *Jek rat, jek jalha, jek dji, jek porh, jek boht.*

"What does it mean?" she asked softly, leaning near. She felt the tremor that shook his powerful body.

"It's an old Romany saying. 'Same blood, same eyes, same soul, one belly, one happiness.'"

"What a beautiful thought."

He looked as if he might say something else, then seemed to change his mind. With effortless grace he continued up the steps and opened the door. When he carried her inside, it was like entering another world. The interior would rival the lavish apartment of a wealthy sultan.

Heather was almost blinded by the kaleidoscope of red, purple and blue satin furnishings. He deposited her among the cushions on the built-in double bed and flashed her a smile. "I feel like a captive princess out of *The Arabian Nights,*" she said breathlessly.

"That's exactly what you are, and I'm never letting you go." His eyes narrowed. He towered over her like some conquering hero and she had a suffocating feeling in her chest. The air seemed charged with tension.

"Please don't tease me, Nick. I . . . I can't take any more."

"And you think I can?" he demanded fiercely. "I still want to know why you wouldn't go with me to see Branko after he came out of recovery."

She clutched the fringe on one of the pillows. "I thought you two needed to be alone."

The quiver in her voice must have betrayed her, because he made a sound of exasperation. "After the way you responded to me in the stairwell, I was convinced you wanted me as much as I wanted you. But when you refused to visit Branko with me, I wasn't certain of anything." He moved closer so she could feel the heat from his body. The breath caught in her throat.

"You must know why I didn't go with you," she said, and scrambled off the bed, anxious to escape before she broke down. Nick had confessed to wanting her, but he had said nothing about love. She reached for the door handle, but Nick was faster and grasped her hand, preventing her from leaving.

"Because you're in love with me? Tell me the truth!" His eyes were black as thunderheads and a hundred times more threatening.

"You know perfectly well I'm so in love with you my whole world has been turned upside down!" Her voice throbbed as she spoke. "For a man of your compassion and instincts, I don't understand why you'd want to continue torturing me when we both know you'll always be in love with Ibra."

"Ibra?" The stunned expression on his face should have told her something was wrong, but she was in too much pain to consider the effect of her words.

Frantically brushing the tears from her cheeks, she cried, "Don't you think I have any feelings at all? That night on the St. Joe, I had to lie there while you told me about her, how you would never have left if you'd known she was pregnant."

"Heather—"

"No," she interrupted, her complexion as drained of color as a piece of alabaster. "Let me finish. You wanted the truth, and if it's embarrassing, I'm sorry.

That's why I didn't want to discuss this, but maybe it's for the best. I'll only be in Branko's life for another ten days. Then none of us will ever have to see each other again.''

Nick's pallor was as pronounced as her own, and the way he clung to her hand felt like a death grip. ''Ibra was my first experience with a woman. It happened right after my parents' death, so I was extremely vulnerable, and flattered by her interest. But after those initial weeks of infatuation, I discovered what a selfish, manipulative person she really was.

''My infatuation with her didn't last long. If it hadn't served my own purposes to go along with her plan to help me escape, I would never have set foot inside her *tsara* again.''

''Aren't you just saying that because she rejected you?'' Heather couldn't refrain from asking, too afraid to believe what she was hearing.

''You're not listening to me,'' Nick said tersely. ''*I'm* the one who did the rejecting, not the other way around. I stopped visiting her *tsara* despite her pleadings.''

Heather's head flew back, causing her hair to flounce around her shoulders. *''You rejected her?''*

''That's right,'' he muttered. ''With hindsight, I can see she got even with me by not telling me she was pregnant. Her scheme to help me achieve my freedom insured her total control over our son. It's true I would never have left Yugoslavia if I'd known about Branko. After witnessing the harsh life of the Gypsies, I would have done everything in my power to obtain custody of him *before* leaving the country. She knew that, and wanted to be able to claim something of her very own."

"But when you were telling me about her on the boat, you sounded heartbroken."

"Because she had robbed me of all those years with my son. And because I felt a deep pity for her." Suddenly his hands were on her shoulders, pressing her back against the door, his eyes like hot flames. "I never truly loved Ibra or any other woman in the intervening years. Not until I met you!"

"Nick..." she said helplessly, the love burning so brightly in her eyes he could have been blinded by it.

Shaking her gently, he said, "You can't imagine the shock it was to find myself in love with the woman Branko had chosen for his wife."

"I think I can," she whispered, sliding her hands over the hard muscled contours of his chest, trying to convince herself this was really happening. "All the time I was angry with you, it was because I was fighting my attraction to you. And the bracelet was constantly between us."

"You know why, don't you?" he asked hoarsely. "It looked as though history had repeated itself. Like father, like son. Branko had found himself an older woman who was the personification of my wildest fantasies. I was terrified. What if you were lying to me and really did want Branko? There were moments when I thought I was going to lose my mind because I wasn't sure of you."

Heather closed her eyes in remembrance. "You were so suspicious I didn't know how to make you see the situation for what it really was."

He shuddered and pressed his forehead to hers. "Oh, I finally saw it, but by then all the damage had been done. I had driven my son away when it was the last thing I ever wanted to do. And to my shame, I coveted his woman. When you roared out of my driveway in righteous indignation, I didn't want to let you go."

"You weren't alone," she confessed, brushing her lips against his cheek. "Somehow my visit had ended up in a nightmare. Meeting you changed my whole life, even though at the time I thought I never wanted to see you again."

"I couldn't stay away from you," he admitted huskily. "Naturally I was sick over Branko's disappearance, but I had to see you again. That night in your classroom was a revelation. While I was following you home, I had this wild impulse to carry you off someplace and make love to you so you'd *have* to belong to me."

"Darling." She raised herself on tiptoe and pressed her mouth to his. He crushed her in his arms, and for the next while the world receded while they gave in to their long-suppressed passion. Nick's hands and mouth became her whole world. His loving made her feel immortal.

"I love you, Heather. Say you'll marry me as soon as possible." He smiled. "Branko has given us his consent."

The words she had been waiting to hear filled her with the greatest happiness she had ever known, but a sharp, sudden pain threatened her joy, and she hid her face in his neck. "I can't give you children, and you deserve to have a baby—lots of them—because you're the most wonderful father I've ever known."

"Listen to me!" He caught her face in his hands and lifted it. "Branko's the biggest baby I know. Agreed?"

She started to laugh in spite of her pain. "But Nick—"

"But nothing. Branko's the son of my body and enough of a child to keep us worried for the rest of our lives. When the grandchildren come, we're going to have our hands full. Besides, Jay told me he's handled several adoptions for childless couples—and he's already working on one for us."

"What?"

He flashed her a wry smile that made him look ten years younger and so handsome it hurt. "Last Sunday night he called to talk. That's when I broke down and told him exactly how I felt about you. In case you have any doubts, he's already welcomed me to the family."

On that note he drew her to the bed, forcing her to lie back so he could lean over her. "What's your answer, my love?" He teased her lips with tantalizing insistence.

His eyes were so translucent she would have seen any shadows if they'd been lurking there. But there were none, and that knowledge filled her universe with sunshine once more.

She traced his mouth with her finger. "I wish I was your wife right now," she confessed, no longer afraid to show or tell him what he meant to her. "Shall we have the ceremony in two weeks? I'll be finished with school by then."

His hand stilled in her hair. "Do you mean that?"

"Can you doubt it?"

On his face was a tremulous, eager excitement that moved her deeply. For the first time since she'd known him, his eyes filmed over. "I swear I'll love you forever."

She stared up at him. "Do you know what Zamura told me?"

"No." He kissed her lips quiet. "What did she say?"

"That a great man had come into my life, a *baro manursh*. That's you, my darling. She said you would take away my sorrow, and that together we would gain all the world has to offer. She also said you would be the only great love in my life. But I already knew that before I went to see her."

"Heather..." His mouth covered hers with smothering force, and once again time had no meaning as Nick began to love her in earnest.

When there was a knock on the door, Heather thought she'd imagined it. The knock grew louder.

"Father?"

Nick groaned and lifted his head, his eyes glazed with unbridled passion. "What is it, Branko?"

"The time. It is six-thirty. Class no have teacher."

"My class! I don't believe it!" she cried while Nick chuckled. "How could I have forgotten?" She tried to pull out of his arms, but he held her firmly, his leg trapping hers.

Nuzzling her ear, he said, "I'll let you go on one condition—that as soon as your class is over, you'll come right back here where you belong. I haven't begun to do what I want with you yet."

"I hope not," she teased, and wriggled to her feet, leaving Nick lounging on the satin spread like a reclining god. It took Heather every ounce of her willpower to walk away from him.

When she opened the door, Branko's curious black eyes darted from Nick's to hers. "You Father's *romni* now?"

A becoming blush swept over her face and neck. Nick grinned at her before saying, "We're getting married as soon as possible." Then he recited the Romany words inscribed over the door of the *tsara*.

"Good." Branko nodded. A glow of satisfaction illuminated his dark eyes, erasing the last lingering doubt in her heart. "Now my father no have other women at house."

After her face fell, Heather realized he had been lying to her about Nick's women from the beginning, and she started to laugh. In the next instant she hugged her soon-to-be-stepson, crutches and all. "Branko Antonovic, how will I ever know when you're serious?"

He shrugged his broad shoulders. "I no understand what you say." He put on the innocent look that she had come to recognize masked his most mischievous behavior.

"Oh, yes, you do," she returned promptly. "You understand everything very, very well."

"Father?" He turned to Nick, who had risen from the bed and was strolling toward them. "Heather is, how you say, one h . . . hell of woman!"

Convulsed with laughter, Nick wrapped his arms around both of them. "Branko, my son, you just said a mouthful."

HARLEQUIN PROUDLY PRESENTS A
DAZZLING CONCEPT IN ROMANCE FICTION

One small town,
twelve terrific love stories.

TYLER—GREAT READING...GREAT SAVINGS...
AND A FABULOUS FREE GIFT

Each book set in Tyler is a self-contained love story;
together, the twelve novels stitch the fabric of
the community.

By collecting proofs-of-purchase found in each Tyler
book, you can receive a fabulous gift, ABSOLUTELY
FREE! And use our special Tyler coupons to save on
your next Tyler book purchase.

Join us for the third Tyler book, WISCONSIN
WEDDING by Carla Neggers, available in May.

HARLEQUIN
Romance®

announces

The Bridal Collection

**one special Romance
every month,
featuring
a Bride, a Groom and a Wedding!**

**Beginning in May 1992
with**
The Man You'll Marry
by Debbie Macomber

WED-1